Alexander Innes Shand

The Lady Grange

Alexander Innes Shand

The Lady Grange

ISBN/EAN: 9783337108991

Printed in Europe, USA, Canada, Australia, Japan

Cover: Foto ©Raphael Reischuk / pixelio.de

More available books at **www.hansebooks.com**

THE LADY GRANGE

BY

ALEXANDER INNES SHAND

AUTHOR OF "KILCARRA: A NOVEL"; "HALF-A-CENTURY; OR,
CHANGES IN MEN AND MANNERS," ETC.

LONDON

SMITH, ELDER & CO., 15, WATERLOO PLACE

1897

BRADBURY, AGNEW, & CO. LD., PRINTERS,
LONDON AND TONBRIDGE.

CONTENTS.

THE LADY GRANGE.

CHAPTER I.

THERE were still stirring times in the Scotland of 1753. The rising of the '15 had been put down; but there were always storm-clouds lowering in the Highlands, which might break at any moment in a descent of the mountaineers. The clans well-disposed to the Crown had submitted to the acts of disarmament, but it was known that arms were hidden, where they could be easily found again, in the wilds of Strathbogie, Badenoch and Lochaber. The military engineering of General Wade had done something towards opening communications, and a straggling chain of forts along the great central glen were held by garrisons of the Sidicor Roy or red-coats. But the Highlands were neither bitted nor bridled. Everything beyond the Highland

B

line was a realm of horror and mystery, where no Lowlander dare risk a foot, except with special protection from one of the high chiefs. These chieftains, with the exception of the wise and war-like MacCullamore, were known to be generally disaffected, or at least open to bribery from the highest bidder in the shape of money or promises. In their own territories their authority was absolute, and they still had the consciences of their clansmen at command for any deed of violence or atrocity. So it was that the unscrupulous Simon of Lovat, whose craft was equalled by his calculating courage, had come to play, perhaps, the most conspicuous part in the events that preceded the catastrophe of Sheriffmuir. So it was that such an almost incredibly dramatic incident was possible as the abduction and life-long sequestration of Lady Grange, when Edinburgh was already *par excellence* the city of the law and the lawyers.

But the explanation of that audacious deed of kidnapping is to be sought in the political circumstances of the Scottish capital, and also in its very characteristic topography. The town, made strongly defensible in troublous times, was crowded on the steep and accentuated ridge which sloped from the castle batteries to the low-lying palace of Holyrood. To the north and south ran an almost perpendicular labyrinth of dark lanes, black closes, and gloomy staircases. As the population increased from the some 40,000 of Mary's reign, the toppling tenements had towered higher and higher. The city was no longer disturbed by the wild broils when the Hamilton and the Douglas, the Leslie and the Seton—see "The Abbot"—fiercely contested the crown of the causeway to the wild gathering cries of followers who were embittered by the memory of many a feud. But in the teeming back-slums and in the swarming rookeries that were safe from the patrols of the superannuated city guards, was hived the most turbulent populace in Europe. So Scott has described them, in telling his story of the Porteous riots. A spark falling among these smouldering combustibles might cause a conflagration at any moment.

The society that formed the upper crust of the slumbering volcano was apparently more tranquil, but the tranquillity was only apparent. Many of the grand seigneurs and solemn statesmen had good reason to take more anxious thought for the morrow than the penniless ruffians in the Cowgate Closes who lived from hand to mouth, and were as ready to sell dirks and souls for a score of marks as any mediæval bravo of Venice or Rome. Intrigue and subtle plot and counterplot had replaced the open violence when—

> "—— the streets of High Dunedin
> Saw lances gleam and faulchions redden."

The centre of political affairs had been transferred to the southern metropolis, but there were still places to be scrambled for, and Walpole's secret service money was none the less welcome, that it was charily remitted. The loaves and the little fishes were all too few for the hungry and importunate claimants. We have seen urchins in the street hustling each other for a handful of coppers; we have seen the shoals of greedy carp in a fishpond splashing and struggling for a scattering of bread—and such was the Edinburgh of 1753. None were satisfied, and most were discontented. The Jacobite emissaries from the shadowy Court of St. Germains were always on the outlook for reckless recruits, and keen for the increase of their credit to compromise men of character and position. Yet the Edinburgh of 1753 was no safe place to conspire in. Even when treason was talked in some tenth-story chamber, looking out across the Frith to Ben Ledi and Benvoirloch, there might be listeners in the floors above or below, and a bird of the air might carry the matter. But when a man was interned in the gloom of one of the odoriferous "lands," a whisper might pass through a chink in the casement to the window of a neighbour, which could be reached with an outstretched arm. Even when the wise and prudent escaped those snares, there were pitfalls in the convivial habits of the time. Ruling elders were as regular in beginning the day with the morning tass of brandy as with family worship. The dinner, that came off soon after high noon, was succeeded by reaming tankards of Bordeaux; and the suppers, which had begun with philosophical discussion, frequently degenerated into carouses or orgies. When the wine was in, the wit went out; and the thinly-veiled treasonable toasts might be succeeded by more outspoken treasonable sentiments. So it was that many a man who professed to glory in unbounded devotion to the reigning dynasty, went about his dignified business with the uneasy conviction that he might have been knotting a halter round his neck in careless moments of dissipation.

Habit is everything, yet it is hard for us to understand how lords and lairds and the cadets of highborn families, could be content to stifle in their dreary dens, where the bairns were packed away in stifling beds, and the solitary sitting-room was a small pannelled parlour. It is true that most of them had some country seat, more or less accessible, whither they could retire in the long vacation, or at other times. But the Scottish country house of 1753, except sometimes for the sake of the scenery, had no great attractions for the men of business or intrigue, who found the zest of their lives in the bustle of society. The old bartizaned tower, built to repel attack and bid defiance to fire, with the narrow windows and loopholes in its massive walls, was gloomy as any of the mansions in the Canongate. Out of doors everything was strictly utilitarian. Sir Walter has confessed himself he made a fancy study of his Tully Veolan. Few of the

Scottish baronial abodes could boast of a superb avenue of horse chestnuts. Fewer still rejoiced in gardens in the French or Dutch style. Generally the "open parks" came to the hall door, and the kail-yard, fringed with a few old-fashioned flowers, was the only attempt at ornamental gardening.

In merry England there were parks and chases, surrounding many a romantic ancestral seat, well stocked with the herds of fallow deer and fenced with their oaken palings. In the Scotch Highlands the parks ranged by the red deer were to be measured by many a rough mountain mile, and the chases, with their vast stretches of seldom-trodden solitudes, covered the better part of many a northern county. But when the Scots had as yet developed little taste for the beautiful, in the Lowlands there were two illustrious exceptions. One was the famous Earl of Mar, who raised the standard of the rebellion in his lordship of Braemar. Mar was a wretched general, but an admirable landscape gardener. The pleasure-grounds at Allon, on which he had lavished untold money, and which before the owner's prescription gave occupation to scores of men, were a vision of beauty and an oasis in the wilderness; the enchanter's wand had created something like the Persian Paradise amid the crooks and the windings of the sluggish Forth.

His younger brother, James Erskine, Lord Grange, shared his tastes and imitated his profession, within the compass of more limited means. The pleasance he had laid out around his house of Preston, in the parish of Prestonkirk, reflected the character of one of the most enigmatical and contradictory of personages. You would have said the pleasance was made to be the retreat of a Drummond of Hawthornden or a Scottish Spencer, whose romantic fancies courted peace and seclusion. There were enticing bowers and shaded alleys and mazes of lovers' walks. The hardy and homely flowers of the North blazed and bloomed in glorious luxuriance amid exotics, protected from the chilling winds from the Firth by hedges of elder matted with the wild briar. Those hedges, with high stone walls behind, screened the gardens of mystery from the gaze of the vulgar. Throughout the week no stranger's foot was suffered to profane the sanctuary. Yet each Sabbath day, from ostentation or philanthropy

or good-fellowship, the gardens were thrown open
to all and sundry. The country folks of Edinburgh, who came to admire, were sorely puzzled
when they took the trouble to think. To some of
them James, Lord Grange, was known as a godly
professor—the lay leader of Ultra-Presbyterians—
whose soul should have risen superior to such
carnal frivolities. There were others, again, who
understood him as the crafty lawyer and scheming politician, and they marvelled that a man so
self-engrossed and subtle should amuse himself
with costly toys to the prejudice of serious in-
terests. While not a few, who saw deeper into
things than their neighbours, would find con-
firmation in the sensuous shades of those alleys of
many a floating calumny and whispered scandal.
No man in Edinburgh, and it is much to say,
had more calumniators and envious back-biters
than that solemn and austere Lord Grange. His
domestic troubles were notorious; and those wise-
acres would shake their heads significantly at the
sight of the little postern door in the enclosing
walls, half-hidden beneath a wealth of honeysuckle
and ivy. It was said to be such a wicket gate as

the discreetly luxurious abbots of the olden time
reserved for the admission of their fairer penitents.
His high-tempered and sharp-tongued lady, the
gossips averred, might have more to say for herself than was generally believed. But Grange was
a man who kept his secrets by making no affectation of mystery. To all outward appearance he
wore his heart upon his sleeve. He was hand in
glove with the most pious divines of the strictest
sect of the Covenanting Communion; and if he
cared to vindicate a spotless character he might
have called up unimpeachable witnesses in clouds.

In one thing both friends and enemies were
agreed. The best of mortals have their failings,
and the most wary may make awkward slips,
especially when troublous days crave wary walking.
The ex-Lord Justice Clerk "drank as other gentlemen do," as the Orkney clergyman said, when
defending himself before the General Assembly
from charges of inebriety. It was rumoured that
conviviality degenerated sometimes into licence, but
for such common indiscretions the best of the
ministers made sympathetic allowance. Yet when
the wine is in, the wit will be out, and not a few

of his friends were apprehensive that the trusted
brother of the chief captain of the Jacobites might
have compromised himself by indiscreet utterances
when the "malt had got above the meal;" or
even by letters inspired by fraternal affection, or by
resentment at the misfortunes which had overtaken
his House. If that shrewish wife of his were
possessed of those secrets—and knowing something
of the man in his weakness, nothing seemed more
likely—what wonder that Grange should look care-
worn and anxious. Had they known more than
they suspected, they might have marvelled at the
man's self-control. In the Sybarite who loved the
indulgences of life, the Puritan who set great store
by the good opinion of the Churches, the politician
who was deep in the black books of Walpole, and was
watching his chance of a revolution of Fortune's
wheel, knew that he was treading among snares and
pitfalls, and that at any hour some trapdoor might
give way under his feet. He shrank from suspense,
he loathed anxiety, yet in day-dreams, as in night-
mares—when the bottle was going its rounds of a
night, or over the small ale that soothed the head-
ache of the morning—in the pew in the church of

St. Giles, or on the judicial bench in the Parliament House, he saw the sword of Damocles suspended by a hair.

He hated his wife as much as he feared her, yet, strange to say, there were moments when he could passionately love her still. One of the most foolish· of his early follies had found him out, and there was an ever-present Nemesis in the truth that his victim had magnetized him. The judge's firm faith in witchcraft and demonology was perhaps confirmed by the superstitious sense of being himself under a magic spell, and when he tardily consented to "soother sin by marriage," he still dreaded the spirit of vengeance incarnate—the only legacy left to a dowerless daughter by the assassin who had expiated his crime on the gibbet.

CHAPTER II.

It was a bright day in bleak December, and the scenery of the Firth of Forth was glittering in wintry splendour. A lady was pacing with hasty steps one of the terraced walks in the gardens of Preston. Though she stopped and looked seawards from time to time, she had no thoughts for the fair scene that stretched before her, from the low-lying Isle of May to the lonely Bass, where the sighs of State captives and the groans of Covenanting martyrs had mingled so often with the screams of the sea-fowl. The lady had the free use of her limbs, but perhaps no prisoner of the Rock, when the irons of the fetters had entered into his soul, had ever showed signs of more passionate impatience. All the more, that like the manacled prisoner, she could only watch and wait in impatience.

"He said he would be here by noon," she

muttered, " and surely the letter must fetch him, and yet the kirk clock has chappit half-an-hour agone."

It was barely ten minutes since the clock had struck, but time goes at a wearisome amble with the impatient.

The woman who was waiting in feverish anxiety must have been very beautiful in youth, and was still strikingly handsome, though more in the style of a Juno than a Venus. The finely-chiselled features had been sharply accentuated by time and care, the cheeks had fallen in, and the complexion had faded. But the pale face, like the chalk cliffs reflecting a revolving electric light, was fitfully illuminated with a sinister radiance by flashes from the great black eyes. If there were a fault in the face, it was a certain unfeminine squareness in the well-moulded chin, and there was a trick of compressing the full lips which, like the flashes from the lustrous eyes, gave significant storm-warnings.

She was dressed with taste and with care, though the material was plain to simplicity. For long the middle-aged beauty—she must have passed the forties, and she looked the age—had made bitter complaint that her scanty pin-money was ever in arrear. She resented being robbed of a woman's best weapons in the warfare she was doomed perpetually to wage with the husband who grudged the supplies. Nevertheless, it was not in her nature to knock under, and she did her best under stress of circumstances. If her gown was of rough homespun, and it was not unsuited to the December temperature, the lappets in the dark locks, shot with silvery streaks, and the trimmings of the swelling bodice were of the rare lace that was a family heirloom. When once the lady had got a grip of anything, to that she held fast. The hair and the lace had been coquettishly arranged, and that morning her tiring-woman had had a hard time of it. But now lace and hair were strangely disordered, for the mistress had clean forgotten her feminine wiles, in the wearying delay of the expected interview.

It need not be said that the excited watcher was the heroine of one of the most melancholy of historical romances. No wonder her husband's friends used to aver that Grange had a grey mare in his stable, and that the grey mare was the better horse. Though there were others who professed doubts on the subject, and maintained that for all Grange's piety and gravity, he was too dangerous a man to make or meddle with. They could add, moreover, with enigmatical significance, that it was ever the quietest water that ran the deepest, that more folk had been drowned in the Fords of Frew than in the brattling Fall of Fayers; and that, when all was said, my Lord Grange had the fiend's own temper, though with grace or years had come the gift to curb it. That he had "a sair handful to deal wi'," in the daughter of Chiesley of Dalry, neither his own friends nor his well-wishers doubted for a moment.

They were right in crediting the wary old lawyer with astute worldly wisdom. After many a sharp passage of arms with his wife, he had become singularly cunning of fence: he had studied his sword-play, he had practised his guards, and was too knowledgeable of her tricks of fence to throw away the slightest advantage. She had given him a pressing invitation for noon on that Saturday. Her reasons for urging the invitation were so vaguely menacing that he durst not decline; but

he would make free to take license as to the hour.
She hoped to assail him when she was comparatively cool and he was fasting. Smiling sardonically, he made thoughtful arrangements for the
hour of his arrival, and when he had drawn on his
boot hose and swung himself into the saddle, he
did not hurry his ambling hackney. He drew rein
at the tavern by Musselburgh bridge for a deep
draught of the Prestonpans ale, though, as Mistress
Dreghorn, the hostess, ruefully remarked, "Grange,
for as great as he was, for the maist part was fond
o' a crack, but he gloomed and girned that morning
as if he had gotten out o' his bed wi' the wrang
leg foremost."

To all appearance, his lordship had recovered
his serenity when he passed through his own gates
at Preston. It was now on the stroke of one : one
was his dinner-hour, and punctuality to the minute
was the rule of the establishment. The sound of
hoofs and the peal of a bell had brought out the
servants to receive the master. There were more
of them than would seem befitting so modest an
occasion: but labour was cheap in those days and
wages were low, and the loons were content to

serve for their keep, with occasional and precarious changes of raiment. So, as the sagacious Grange had foreseen, the greetings with his lady were exchanged in public. On his part they were boisterously hearty and effusively affectionate. Yet, with the domestics looking on, there was something of stately ceremony in the kiss he imprinted on her burning cheek. She had self-restraint enough to mutter an acknowledgment, but if looks could have killed the laggard, he would have fallen dead on his threshold. In his genial flow of spirits he would see nothing.

"I am come fasting from all save sin, and half-frozen to the back of that. Set on the dinner with as small delay as may be. Your pardon, Rachel, while I shift my riding-gear. Heap on the logs in the ingle-neuk. You, Peter, come your ways with me, and lend a helping hand."

And so the impending *tête-à-tête* was deferred. Though the windows were small and the walls were thick, the pannelled dining parlour was a cheerful room. It is true that the family portraits on the walls presented for the most part rather forbidding personages. There were grim warriors

of the Erskines sheathed in mail, austere statesmen in frizzled periwigs, wooden-faced dowagers in
starched ruffs. But fuel was cheap in those parts,
and the great blaze went roaring up the ample
chimney, flashing bright reflections from the
polished wainscotting. The solid table groaned
beneath the substantial fare, and there were made
dishes as well as ponderous joints, for Grange had
graduated at the table of his brother, and was a
Gourmand and a connoisseur in French cookery.
The "napery," though coarse, was of spotless
white, if the garnishing of the buffet left something
to desire, and there was but a meagre show of plate
and crystal. Anxiety did not appear to have im-
paired his appetite. Lord Grange was known for
a famous trencherman, and within reach of his
hand was a flagon filled with claret fresh drawn
from the hogshead. He ate deliberately, and drank
deep. Some men would have held back from the
wine, knowing the delicate business before them;
but Grange was a seasoned vessel, and could flood
himself in Bordeaux with impunity. When it
came to the brandy, and in good company towards
the small hours, then, indeed, in common prudence,

he might have acted more wisely had he been in the
habit of calling a halt!

Lady Grange scarcely pretended to trifle with
the dishes, but she did not shrink from the wine.
The conversation, which was seldom lively at the
best of times, soon dropped. From time to time,
my lord, industriously plying knife and fork, would
steal a furtive glance at my lady—sometimes
addressing a remark to Peter over his shoulder.
She was evidently working herself up to fever-pitch,
and he foreboded a phenomenal storm. Would it
break, as it generally did, and clear the air, or this
time would it leave wreck and ruin behind. He
apprehended the worst, and was preparing for the
emergency.

The dinner was over, the cloth was removed, a
fresh supply of claret was placed on the table,
and the domestics had withdrawn. The door was
barely closed before the lady burst forth.

"Now, my lord, you will please to favour me
with your attention."

"Surely, sweetheart, what else did I come for,
when by rights I should have been in the town on
pressing affairs that are ill to hold over? Forbye,

that there are few husbands who would have drawn
on their boots to ride to Preston when the curling
stanes were rolling on Duddingstone. But, in truth,
there is no fool like an auld fool, and weel ye know
ye could always twine me round your fingers,
Rachel. And bonny fingers they are!"

·Perhaps he felt he owed it to himself to try the
flattery, which, with its awakening of sentimental
associations, had often succeeded before. On this
special occasion he could have hoped little from it.
The atmosphere was surcharged with electricity,
the lightnings were flashing from the wild black
eyes, and the storm was bound to break. Yet, as a
prelude to the main attack and the grand engage-
ment, came a characteristic touch of feminine
spite.

"My bonny fingers! and so it's because they're
so bonny that they're set off neither with diamonds
nor rubies, as they should be. My bonny fingers,
and the bonny face that has cost me sae dear!
Well ye know that mair than twenty lang years of
sorrow have shrivelled the one and saddened the
other. But the cup ye have been filling overflows,
and now ye shall drain it to the dregs."

It was not so much the expected abuse as the look of deadly malignity which accompanied it that startled Grange. He knew his wife's temper well; he had good reason to dread the violence he had often experienced; but never before had he seen her so deeply moved and seemingly so fixed on some sinister resolution. The searchings of a troubled conscience sent the shivers to his very marrow.

"What is the matter, woman?" he exclaimed, starting to his feet and upsetting the claret flagon. "What may be in the wind with you now, Rachel?" he went on more softly, and making an effort to calm himself.

"'What is the matter?' do ye say? 'What's in the wind?' and ye have the front to ask me? Do ye happen, ken that hand?"

She held out to him a soiled and crumpled scrap of paper. Grange took it and glanced at the brief contents, for there was no superscription. His lordship was long past blushing, but he certainly looked taken aback.

"Here's a glint of moonshine in the water—a work, about a line or two, written in all honour and honesty to a poor bit lass that might be my daughter."

"Your daughter—aye, or your grand-daughter, as ye might say. What have ye to do, at your time of life, with chambering and wantonness, with writing and making trystes with ill-living hussies in the upper chambers of ill-faured ale-houses. It well beseems you that were a judge of the land, and the Lord Justice Clerk to boot. It would have better befitted ye to send siccan limmers to the Tolbooth to dree the hangman's lash. And will ye dare to deny now that I was in my rights when I bid ye wall up that wicket door in the Pleasaunce?"

"Canny, canny, my lady! I give you my honour as a gentleman you're clear mistook. The lassie's father is a decent man, a good-living deacon of the kirk, and I was only wishing to get her well put out in the world."

"And so she came seeking for the place after dark, when ye were supping with Simon Fraser at Luckie Dreghorn's."

"See now, Rachel, how your Satan-begotten jealousy is turning your brain. I bid the lass come when Simon was supping with me, that I might shun the mere suspicion of scandal."

"A fine companion is Lovat to pass warrant for

a lass's character, if a' tales be true that come from Castle Downie. I know well, James, that I might be content to bide my time, for you will assuredly be damned for a sanctimonious Pharisee: aye, you'll burn eternally, that's sure enough ; but the hottest neuk in hell would be ower cold for Simon Fraser. And if this Lizzie Gilmour had never lived, think you I have forgotten or overlooked your other ill-doings? But to give the Devil his righteous due, that Satan from Strath Beauly is at the bottom of all the trouble. He draws you on to drink, and to drab, and maybe to dice— what ken I—I know that the siller is always lacking here. He plays on your follies and your feebleness like the strings of a fiddle ; fine music you make between you, and it's like to end with tows and halters in a fair dance, as you will find."

Grange prided himself on no ordinary self-control, but for once he was roused out of patience and temper. His wife's savage onslaught had stung him doubly. When she roundly abused him for a Pharisee she touched a chord that always vibrated painfully. No one could have told half so much as himself of the man who made clean the outside of the platter. And when she spoke of Lovat playing on his foibles, she said nothing more than the simple truth. Boasting even to himself of strength of will and profound worldly wisdom, he knew that he ever turned for counsel to the Highland Achitophel, and that when it came to a discussion over ways and means, it was the purpose of Lord Lovat that always prevailed. Possibly, had he still striven to turn away anger with soothing words, this storm might have blown over like many before, and the impending catastrophe might again have been averted. But in the turmoil of passions tempestuously stirred, and heated with the wine, he gave the rein to his temper. He might have taken it as a sinister sign, that as he grew more excited his wife calmed down. He threatened, and she turned deaf ears to his threats: already she was enjoying an instalment of her vengeance. It would have been well for her, and none the worse for him, had she been satisfied to listen in sullen silence. But she could not resist the temptation of the last word, of answering menace with menace. Bracing herself up with the dignity of a tragedy

queen, she pointed a warning finger to the door
and the keyhole. Recalled to the instincts of
prudence and self-preservation, Grange dropped his
voice, and his threatenings died away in inaudible
murmurs. His wife, following up her advantage,
stepped across to him, and whispered or hissed in
his ear. As he listened, his face, flushed with passion and the draughts of claret, turned deadly pale.
He made an effort to answer, but was silenced by
a choking in the throat, unpleasantly suggestive of
the tightening of a halter. Before he recovered
his voice and some measure of composure, his
amiable helpmate had swept out of the room.
Going to the buffet, he swallowed a bumper of
brandy, and then sank down into the high-backed
oaken chair, the seat of dignity in the shadow of
the mantelshelf. But there was little semblance
of dignity about the grave Lord of Justiciary.

CHAPTER III.

WHEN the lady left her lord, his reflections were disagreeable enough. But the low-ceilinged room, with its closed windows, was warm; he had dined heavily and drunk freely, and he soon sunk to sleep in his chair. In his sleep he tossed and turned, and he woke up feverish and unrefreshed in the worrying sense of impending calamity. The natural resource of a Scottish gentleman of the period was to ring and call for more brandy. The old serving-man who helped him from the buffet seemed to linger, as if not unwilling to be questioned.

"And what the deevil may *you* be waiting for, that I should say so?" burst out his master.

"Naething, naething, my lord; for doubtless your lordship is aware that her ladyship has made a flitting o' it."

Surprised alike out of prudence and propriety,

Grange broke into an execration, which was answer sufficient. So the servant took it, and went on. The man had been in the household from his youth up, and in his way was attached to his master. But he was curiously inquisitive, like all his tribe, and leading habitually the dullest of lives, he could not miss the lucky chance of making the most of a sensational incident. More by token, as he shrewdly suspected, for once he was better instructed than Lord Grange.

"Aye, the lady has taken coach for the lodging in the Lawnmarket, and it's likely she purposes to go a bittock further."

"Will ye speak out, man, and be damned to you," exclaimed Grange, still half-confused by his broken slumbers. Then, reminded by the servant's face how entirely he stood committed, he thrust his hand into the pocket of his broidered waistcoat, drew forth a piece of gold, and held it out.

"Keep a quiet tongue, Peter, for it concerns the honour of the family. Be silent, I mean, to all but me, and now go on and make a clean breast of it."

"Na, na!" said Peter, putting his itching hand behind his back in an act of self-abnegation, for seldom had he handled aught save silver. "Na, na! my lord, I hae eaten o' your bread and drunken o' your cup, nor am I free to sell my lady for siller. But my first and bounden duty is to yoursel', and so ye're welcome to hear all I can tell ye. The rather," he added, by way of post-script, "that it was never the mistress' pleasure to trust me."

The long and the short of the story was, that the mistress had been making up her mails the day before.

"And, as I jalouse, she was ever in a double mind, and waiting for your lordship to come, to tell how the wind might be setting. Her plans laid, she had but to send to Musselburgh to fetch the coach, and so the stable lad went off, when she came out from the dining parlour."

"But what was your meaning when you said that she might, maybe, be going farther?"

"Just this—as your lordship knows, the women will aye be chattering, and her tirewoman, for as close as she has been keeping her lips, chanced to let slip a word about her ladyship having taken a place in the stage for London. Whereupon, as in duty bound, I made divers speerings, but the thrawn jade would answer no questions. That is all I can tell, were they to put me in the boots or the finger-screws, and it's for your lordship's wisdom to make the best or the worst of it."

The man was dismissed with almost affectionate thanks and another solemn injunction of secrecy. Grange was left again to meditation, and his latter condition was far worse than the first. That wife of his was the daughter of Chiesley of Dalry, whose cruel deed of long-calculated revenge had rung through the length and breadth of Scotland. Dalry had died not only impenitent, but glorying in his revenge. Rachel was his true daughter; she had sorrowed for her father, but had never blamed him. On Rachel he had inflicted the deepest wrong that man can inflict on woman. True, he had redressed it in the eyes of the world by a tardy marriage, and even now it shamed him to remember how that unwelcome marriage had been forced upon him. It had been settled in a stormy scene, which nearly ended in

a bloody tragedy. He might have still loved his
fiery mistress—in fact, there were times when he
was touched by the old feelings, which were fiercely
ardent rather than tender, but the links of the
forced wedlock had fretted him intolerably. To
be sure, he wore them loosely, and in his frequent
visits to the South they imposed slight restraint
on him. Those scandals, unbelieved or at least
contradicted by his good allies of the kirk, were
wafted to the North. There were violent letters of
reproach from Edinburgh or Preston, presaging
the storm that awaited the wanderer on his home-
coming. "Anything for a quiet life" had ever
been his motto, and he had sought to avert the
crisis of the morrow by drawing dubious bills on a
distant future. When fair words, false oaths, and
caresses had failed, in maudlin moods between his
fears and the wine flasks, he had sought to disarm
his domestic Fury by proofs of his absolute confidence. As experience had shown, that was the
only way of temporarily tiding over his troubles.
And now he trembled to think of the perilous
secrets which might have escaped him. For aught
he knew or could remember, he might have signed

his death-warrant by insanely setting his hand to some compromising paper. And his wife was the daughter of Chiesley, the assassin! But Grange was used to treading among pitfalls, and reflection brought a calmer and more philosophical mood. This storm, threatening as it was, might blow over like the others. "Anyhow, it would be worse than bootless, running after the wilful woman in her maddest mind. And let me see—aye, the next conveyance for the South does not set out till the Saturday. In the meantime, I'll be none the waur for company and counsel."

He turned to a table, dashed off a note, and rang again.

"See that this line is sent up forthwith to the manse."

For the veteran politician had two standing advisers, though the one was far deeper in his confidence than the other. The worthy minister of the parish of Prestonpans, if not exactly the keeper of his conscience, was his wonted adviser in things spiritual. It was agreeable to feel that in discussing delicate questions, he could play the Balak to the clergyman's Balaam, and put a

certain pressure on that excellent man. Of course
the reverend gentleman was not to be swayed by
the hope of being transferred to a more lucrative
benefice, or of having revisions of the tiends
arranged to his advantage by the law-lord, who
was likewise his principal heritor. But still——

The relations of the strangely-assorted friends
were so remarkable, that they would seem incredible were they not matter of historical certainty.

John Knox and the zealous apostles of the
Reformation had sown seed which had struck deep
root, though in a rude and unkindly soil. The
Lords of the Congregation were the descendants
of the fierce and warlike barons, who, in their
petty divisions, had been laws unto themselves.
With the right of pit and gallows over defenceless
dependents, they had no public opinion to fear.
As Catholics, they had purged their souls periodi-
cally by confession, and wiped out their awkward
reckonings with heaven by deathbed donations at
the expense of their heirs. Most of them accepted
the Protestant faith because they enriched themselves by gifts of confiscated Church lands. Even
Knox himself found it difficult or impossible

D

to deal with such worldly-minded nobles as the politic but dissipated Morton. The ministers of the new creed might pray and preach, but with the disadvantages of their poverty and inferior social position, they were too often constrained to hold a candle to the devil. They tolerated what they could not forbid; and the nobles who listened to long extempore prayers, in place of hearing a short hunting mass, still indulged in all manner of licence. Of course there were not a few exceptions, who carried piety and asceticism to extreme lengths, and whose conduct and example were not without their weight. With the advance of civilization and the strengthening of the law, the aristocracy lost its feudal rights of hereditary jurisdiction, became more amenable to opinion, or paid it the tribute of some outward observance. The middle and lower classes in Lowland Scotland have always been so profoundly religious that their zealous sincerity had necessarily led to the multiplication of hypocrites and formalists. Men in the highest places had found it their interest to appear sanctimonious. Not unfrequently habitual sinners actually lived in the terror of Judgment to come

and some vague hope of eternal felicity. But the
habits of the class and age were not only convivial
but licentious. The flesh and the world prevailed
over the spirit. There were godly professors, who,
like the Fifth Monarchy fanatics of the English
civil wars, believed that predestination and full
future assurance permitted them present indulgence, for to the pure all things were pure. It is
to be supposed that Lord Grange held the fatal
faith, although there were times when he was
troubled with grave misgivings, and on that theory
only can his inconsistencies be explained.

The minister of Prestonpans was well used to
these sudden invitations and always glad to obey
them. As a rule, they began with meat and talk;
were carried on with the outpourings of fervent
prayer, and ended, as they had commenced, with
drinking. On this occasion the Rev. Dr. Wiseman
found his noble patron preoccupied and taciturn.
The good man really took a kindly interest in him,
although concern did not interfere with appetite.
But when he had done justice to the well-spread
supper-table, curiosity and interest got the upper
hand, and he waxed impatient.

"Will your lordship not mix yourself a tumbler?" said the minister, setting the example. His lordship sighed, groaned, and complied. Then taking his resolution, he plunged *in medias res.*

"I would seek your opinion, my excellent friend, on a case of conscience, and this it is. You know yourself, and none better, that I have been cursed with a camsteary and contrary wife. You know how I have borne and endured with the thorn in the flesh sent to buffet me, for many a time have we striven together on our knees for help. I can put up, as I have done, with the sorrow and the smart, but now—the ill's like to prove mortal."

"If I am to advise," said the minister, after a pause, "your lordship must be more explicit."

"Altogether explicit I cannot be, though I trust in you as my friend and father in the faith, for there are matters that concern others beside me. But you may take for certain, doctor, that this time the rights are with me, and all the wrongs with her. It is a great affair of state and of high kirk policy to boot. She has taken offence without the shadow of a cause—or, anyhow, with no sufficient reason, and she threatens my liberty, if not my

life—my lands and my goods, and, maybe, my
honour.   And now, minister, the woman is in
deadly earnest—an incarnate fury, this day, if ever
there was one; and mind ye, she's the daughter of
Dalry."

The minister pursed up his lips, wrinkled his
brow in evident dubiety, and waited to hear more.

"Its a case of conscience, I say, and far more
than a question of self-preservation.   The woman's
gone mad—clean mad—I might sue out a brief to
bring her in *furiosa*, and have her handed over to
safe and lawful keeping.   But, in the meantime,
there would be no bridling of her tongue; she's
capable, in her tantrums, of swearing to anything.
Moreover, minister, if I must tell the naked truth,
there are certain material proofs, which my enemies
in the Courts and the Holoferneses who would make
havoc of the kirk, might wrest to the aid of their
malignant purposes."

"And ye can aver on soul and conscience that
ye stand free from blame in this special matter."

"Clear and clean of anything beyond the sins
of my youth, that I have confessed and striven
my utmost to atone for."

" But what would you wish to do, Grange? and what is the question you are to put to your pastor? "

" Just this, and I would have it well settled to my mind, before I seek to other and worldly counsel. Would it be lawful and right to have this unhappy lady put out of the way of doing a mischief, by imperilling the State and making scandal among the godly, without asking for the interference of the law? "

" Ye could not—ye could not—"

" Nothing of the kind, man—nothing of the sort, it would seem, ye are hinting at. God forbid, that, to prolong my days, or even for the sake of the tabernacle, or the Ark of the Covenant, I should lay upon my soul the stain of blood-guiltiness. Besides, man, there are whiles when I love the woman yet, and if she had only had the sense to wink a bit in place of being blinded and besotted with jealousy, she might have been sleeping peaceably the night in her bed up the stairs, and you and me might have been having our cracks over other matters. Not for all the wealth this world could give, would I sin deliberately beyond hope of

forgiveness. The most that I meant was mild and
temporary restraint—sequestration with due consideration and respect, in some place where she
would be treated with all tenderness."

And the upshot of the preliminary consultation
was that the clergyman, cautiously leaving to the
judge the responsibility for a frank exposition of
the case, gave his opinion that it was not only
lawful but advisable that the ill-guided woman who
had wantonly made herself a stone of stumbling
and a rock of offence, should be deprived for a time
of the opportunities of doing mischief.

"As ye would coerce a raving lunatic in a braced
waistcoat—to be taken off when she returned again
to her right mind."

CHAPTER IV.

FRIENDS IN COUNCIL.

HAD the lady known of her husband's consultation with his ghostly adviser, she would probably have cared little. She had a supreme contempt for the cloth herself, nor could she understand fine drawn samples of conscience. But the agitation in which she reached Edinburgh would have been aggravated had she recognized a tall and stately elderly gentleman who made way for her coach in the crush of the Canongate. Her husband, who followed her to the town the next day, saw a very special interposition of Providence in the message awaiting him at his lodgings. The Lord Simon of Lovat had arrived from the North, and would be glad if Grange would sup that night at "Fortune's."

"A special interposition of Providence, indeed!" Each hour was precious before the starting of the London coach—and Lovat, to whom he would have turned for counsel or help, as he fancied, was far

away, on the banks of the Beauly. And here was
his Highland confidant at hand—and surely he *was*
sent by Providence and not by Satan. Grange felt
as if he had been lightened of a load of care.

The scene of their meeting that evening would
have seemed strange enough to modern men of
fashion. The favourite resort of those high-born
and high-placed gentlemen was mean and miserable
to squalor. The walls and roof were begrimed
with smoke, the greasy planks of the floor creaked
to each movement of the foot, the dismal chamber
was doubtfully lighted by a couple of tallow candles
guttering in their tin sconces, the clothless table
was rough and the chairs were rickety, the claret
was served in pewter stoups, in keeping with the
battered sconces. Yet there was no mistaking the
air of breeding and birth in the sexagenarian cronies
who had sat down to face each other. Grange was
tall and fair, grave and somewhat portly—such a
burgomaster, versed at once in commerce and politics
as Holbein or Van der Helst might have painted.
But even a careless observer would have turned from
him at once to the more striking presence and personality of his companion. The Highland chieftain

was not a handsome man; there was something of
the Highland harshness in the high cheek-bones, and
either naturally or by some misadventure the nose
was broken and flattened. But there was no mistaking the celebrated Simon of Lovat for a common
man; and with the long silvery locks which he wore
falling over his shoulders in eccentric fashion, at first
sight and with his features in repose, he had an air
of patriarchal dignity. A flurried woman in distress would have cast herself impulsively on his
protection. In calmer mood she might have hesitated, and she would have shrunk from him in
terror had she chanced to see him in anger. If a
Holbein might have done justice to Grange, Lovat
would have lent himself to the brushes of Velasquez,
whose genius read the souls of his subjects and
stamped on the features a reflex of the mind. The
great Spaniard would have caught the sinister
glitter in the eyes, contracting in passion like an
angry cat's, and the flexible contraction of the thin
lips, closing fast upon the teeth in the broad mouth
like the jaws of a spring-trap. Our own Hogarth
has preserved the expressive face. The patriarch,
long accustomed to the abuse of arbitrary power, was

more apt to forget himself than when a friendless adventurer, although he had grown grey in the practices of guile and hypocrisy.

Grange and Lovat were birds of a feather, but it was a case of the eagle matched against the cunning hooded crow. Yet, unlike the crow, Grange had a sort of a conscience, though a very conformable one. Lovat had neither conscience nor moral sense, and the only sentiment which had the character of a virtue seems to have been a patriarchal longing for the devotion of his clan. For his courage we may say that it was equal to his craft—his imperturbable coolness seldom failed him; and in the last extremity when the catastrophe of Culloden had banished him once more to the heather and the bracken, he was the only man among the panic-stricken and desperate Jacobites who kept his head and devised a plan which might possibly have secured them tolerable terms.

Never, perhaps, has any man had stranger experiences. He had headed bands of caterans in his wilds of Strathcuick, and held his own as a master of subtlety with the most sagacious diplomatists of England and France. When it suited him, he could

assume the air of homely simplicity, which baffled
and misled the most keen-sighted. He had lived
in Scotland for good part of his life, a hunted out-
law with a price on his head, and all the time was
in correspondence with the leaders of the Government and the Opposition. He had ventured to
London, with a death sentence hanging over him,
and he was only in safety in the midst of his own
clansmen, whom he ruled, nevertheless, with an iron
rod. His statecraft knew how to conciliate their
prejudices, yet any individual who offended him was
either swung up to the gibbet, or consigned to the
cavern-dungeons in his fortalice, where they could
hear the jovial revelry in the halls above. For
it was from Lovat's free-handed and far-sighted
hospitality that Scott undoubtedly sketched to the
life Fergus MacIvor's reception of Waverley at
Glennaquoich.

The Highland riever who had driven cattle, kid-
napped and imprisoned high-born ladies, and laid
successful ambushes for formidable feudal enemies,
ventures to King William's Court at Loo to sue out
a pardon in person. In various disguises, and
sometimes by use of sword and pistol, he makes

his way from Loo to St. Germains—of all places—
passing through a country swarming with com-
batants, where any suspicious wayfarer was summarily shot for a spy. He safely treads the tight
rope between the factions at St. Germains, though
his welcome by the Dutch usurper might have been
supposed an indifferent recommendation. When the
great king at Versailles was so fenced in by ceremo-
nial and etiquette, that Montmorencys and Rohans
found access difficult, the Scottish adventurer has the
private entry, and is admitted to sundry confidential
interviews. He was as much at home in lace and
ruffles as in the ragged trews and brogues; and he
changed his creed as easily as his costume. It is a
fact that he took orders in the Catholic Church, and
administered the most solemn rites of religion with
characteristic unction. In spite of all his shiftings, at
last he was laid by the heels and sent to confinement
under a *lettre de cachet*. It was the interest of many
a powerful enemy to keep him a prisoner, but the trap
was never made to hold the man who had the wiles
of his own mountain foxes. And though his grey
head fell to the headsman in the end, he lived in
fame, if not in honour, to the full four-score and ten.

Report had magnified his audacious exploits, and they never lost anything by his own narration. The craft and unscrupulousness with which he was credited in a crafty and unprincipled age inspired an almost superstitious terror. No man had ever got really the better of him, and when conspiracies were disclosed of which he was the soul, subordinates and accomplices were sure to be the scapegoats. Yet he always continued to maintain a certain credit; he could fascinate men and women alike, and he managed to make staunch friends of such statesmen as Forbes of Culloden. Trusted by some, hated by many, and feared by all, his friendship was almost as fatal as his enmity. He never forgave nor forgot a slight or an injury; and yet, when it suited his immediate purpose, he would actually be an unfeigning friend for the time, letting the account stand over for future settlement. Such was the man from whom Grange sought advice and assistance in his domestic difficulty, and Lady Grange would have surely found some means of leaving the capital immediately had she known that Achitophel was closeted with her husband.

The allies met with a boisterous greeting. Then Lovat, with a twinkle of the cold grey eyes, drew in his chair and bent over the table, filling a bumper and pledging his companion. Walls have ears, old panelling has perilous chinks, and the creaking stairs of rickety tenements are pregnant with suspicion to schemers and plotters.

"And now, James, my man, we had best be buckling to your business."

Grange looked an enquiry.

"I had matter in plenty to talk about, but that will keep. If I am not the more mistaken, your own affairs are the most pressing. I can see trouble in your wrinkles writ in the biggest of print. To think that an old sneck-drawer of a lawyer should show his mind in his face like a school-callant. An ill habit, my lord, between the best of friends. But out with it, man. It's the auld story, I assume. The wife has been driving the swine again through your hanks of yarn."

For answer, Grange stooped nearer his companion and murmured his story. For some time the old cynic listened complacently and chuckled sardonically. Then Grange lost patience and temper. Bringing his lips nearer to the other's withered cheek, he whispered something, with a gleam of malicious satisfaction, which moved Lovat strangely.

" You will never tell me you were mad enough for that, my lord ? "

" I do tell you so," said Grange, doggedly, " and ye may make the best and the worst of it. We are in the same ship again, as we have been together in many another besides, and with the squall that's sure to blow up from the South, it will need your pilotage, and maybe more, to bring us safe into harbour."

The cynical suavity of face changed to a diabolical grimace. Though Grange had long been familiar with his friend, he shank back from the malignant glitter of the contracted eyes. Lovat drummed on the table with his talon-like claws, and if looks could have killed, Grange would have been sped. In that brief period of swift reflection, what a tumult of tempestuous thought swept through Lovat's scheming brain. For already he was bracing himself for the emergency and devising means of extrication. The plans of long years of patient time-serving, the ambitions which had been the fond dreams of his life, and for which he had perilled salvation—for Lovat, like Grange, had his religious moods—all placed at the mercy of a mad woman! And this uxorious idiot at his elbow, whom he had been fool enough to trust with his secrets. Well, many a time before, he had been his own worst enemy; the folly was his, and he must find the remedy. He smoothed his brow and softened his speech.

"Well, well, the mischief's done, and we must seek out some way to mend it. Fill up your glass, James, and drink to our happier future. And, so you say, she leaves the day after the morrow?"

"As luck would have it, there was no place in the coach. She cannot set out till to-morrow se'nnight."

"The Lord be praised!" ejaculated Lovat, fervently; and he filled and tossed off a bumper of the Bordeaux, with a sigh of relief. "A week is an eternity, man. Anoint your head and wash your face, and cast off the garments of heaviness, for, in the speech of your canting councillors, you have been vouchsafed a crowning mercy you never

E

deserved." The old intriguer seemed actually exhilarated by the sense of an imminent danger with assurance of the means of escape.

"Hark ye, James," and in his turn he stooped to whisper. Even a listener looking over their shoulders could scarcely have overheard the words spoken with muttered emphasis—"She must be silenced, and soon. She maun be disposed of."

Grange appeared to protest and object. The conversation, with both speaking eagerly and simultaneously, became animated, even angry. As they grew excited they became less regardful of prudence, and the imaginary eavesdropper might have heard more.

"I tell you," said Lovat, with stern insistence, "this is no time for qualms or scruples. The matter is out of your hands and mine, my lord, for we owe a solemn duty to trusting friends. It is not for you to hold back, who have been knotting the nooses for our necks." And then, changing his mood, like the weather of a West Highland day—

"You're devilish scrupulous, James, for a Lord of

Justiciary and the Chief Justice to boot, who has
many a time set on the black cap as if he were
cocking his beaver for a canter in the King's Park.
Strafford proved himself a fool in the end, but he
only spake God's truth when he said 'Stone dead
hath no fellow.' But have it your own way, if you
will; and if you be frighted at what would, when
all was said and done, be only an extra-judicial act
of justice, not to speak of state-policy, we must
seek for another way out of the wood. What will
ye say now to a burying, without even a death-bed
or a corpse?"

Then the voices sank again, and the whispering
went forward as before.

"On my soul, man, not a hair of the woman's
head shall be harmed."

"I would I could be assured of that."

"On my soul, on my conscience! by the honour
of my House, I, Simon of Lovat, give you my personal guarantee."

Grange shook his head, then, looking his formidable ally full in the face, he nerved himself to take
the Highland bull by the horns.

"You and I are too old acquaintances, Simon,

for you to try to draw me with straws like that. And I would I knew the oath that could bind you."

"I'll swear it on my dirk and the Bible. I'll swear it by all that man holds dear—by my trust in God—by my assurance of salvation."

Again they muttered and argued for a time, when Grange met the outstretched hand of Lovat with a hesitating clasp that clinched the bargain.

Then the wily chieftain cleared his brow, snapped his fingers over his head, and burst out with real or feigned joviality. He prided himself, by the way, on familiarity with the classics. "*Pellite curas*, James, whistle the worries down the wind; fill up your glass, and give us the latest news from the South, of his Grace of Argyll, and of my Lord of Islay."

The clock of the Tron had long struck twelve, when the well-matched friends shook hands and parted. Grange made his way home to his lodgings, through dark closes and ill-paved streets, with uncertain steps. Even had not all respectable citizens been snug in bed, it would have been nothing unusual to see a Lord of Session, or a doctor of divinity, somewhat unsteady after a convivial supper. And that evening his lady had been sitting in her lodgings looking out upon the storm-clouds banking up from the north, nursing her wrath, and gloating on the vengeance that seemed as sure as any wrathful woman could desire.

CHAPTER V.

A DEATH AND A BURIAL.

THREE days later, Lovat was seated in his chamber at breakfast. The powdered beef, the fowls, and the fishes were flanked by a foaming tankard of strong ale and a tall flask of French brandy. His lordship always looked well to the vivers and his creature comforts, and he supped heartily the night before he went to the scaffold. His buxom landlady, who claimed cousinship with the Frasers, and her blooming daughters, were at his beck and call. The cramped quarters and the homely service were in strange contrast with the barbaric state at Castle Downie, where he had more obsequious attendants than he could easily find food for. But here, in the Southland capital, it was very different. The lavish lord of many a barren league, and some square miles of fat acres around Inverness, was constrained to economy that trenched upon niggardliness. The few gold pieces in a lean purse scarcely

sufficed to make a decent show, though eked out by
precarious remittances from London and St. Germains. Nevertheless, even in these lofty lodgings
in the Lawnmarket, the chieftain still kept a sort
of court; there were gentlemen of the clan in waiting on the stairs, who were received with stately
ceremony, and felt honoured by an interview with
MacShimei. Round the close-head below lounged a
tattered tail, eager to receive and obey his behests.
There were desperadoes who had found the North
too hot for them, or who had come South in the
flattering hope of mending their humble fortunes,
and mingled with them were men who got a doubtful
living, nominally as cadies or messengers. They
carried the golf clubs of lawyers and burgesses, they
were in attendance to lend an arm to their patrons
when they staggered home after a prolonged carouse.
In short, they were always ready to run errands for
all and sundry, willing panders to the wills of their
betters who could pay, and yet wearing such an air
of grave respectability that their demeanour might
have deceived the very elect. So that if MacShimei
were meditating any dubious piece of work, there was
no lack of fitting instruments to do his bidding.

On this particular morning, anyone who knew his lordship well might have surmised that he was expecting tidings of importance. With the two or three familiars admitted to his levée, there was no reason to play the hypocrite. In some shape they were bound to him, soul and body; even in Edinburgh, the production of a damning piece of evidence might send them to the Tolbooth, and thence to the gibbet. They might be scathless and sackless in the eye of the law, but they feared the chieftain as much as they reverenced him.

No courier arrived red-footed from the North, no packet, doubly sealed and secured, came by secret envoy from the English metropolis, but as he impatiently tossed off another glass of brandy, a note was brought in by the lad who lay in waiting without his door and superseded the necessity for a bell. He tore it open and read it, and a smile stole over his features. " Tell Foster and Inverallochy that I desire their presence," he said; and for an hour or more he was closeted with a couple of gentlemen of his suite, who enjoyed and fully deserved his confidence.

If he read the expected missive with a cynical smile, it was nevertheless of serious import, and should have awakened all his sympathy for an afflicted friend. Lord Grange had written in sore distress; no communication could have been more decorously worded. Produced in any law plea in any court of justice, it must speak volumes for the good feeling of the writer. Grange hastened to acquaint his old friend and gossip of the domestic bereavement impending. His lady had been suddenly struck by some fell disease—apoplexy or paralysis—a deplorable temper had at last got the better of her; the family physician had passed sentence, and she could not survive for many hours. "God knows," he added, pathetically, "that the blow will fall heavy on me, though few ken better than yourself, Simon, of the bitter crook in my lot. I have suffered much and I have greatly forborne, enduring recrimination and ill-founded suspicion. Even now, when she left my house in an unworthy blaze of ill-jealousy, I hurried up after her to explain and expostulate. But it seemed as if the poor woman, the daughter of Dalry, was possessed with a very devil, and this is the upshot. God,

Simon, you may not believe it, for I fear that the world lies ower near to your heart; but I cannot and never will forget the days when Rachel Chiesley was far more than life to me, and it would be little to give my lands to have her back again as she used to be."

Lovat had read and chuckled approval. Had his friend's communication been differently worded, it would have been worth while to treasure it against contingencies. As it was, it was too dexterously drawn to be worth the keeping, and, on the whole, he preferred to answer it in person.

The sudden death of Lady Grange made no inconsiderable sensation. Necessarily scandal and gossip ran their course, but there was no affectation of secrecy to add fuel to the fire. The doctor in attendance, a *protégé* and creature of the Erskines, was eager to be interviewed right and left, for it meant endless tasses of brandy. After all, his story was a simple one—the attack was sudden, the result inevitable, and there was neither time nor need to call in further assistance. The whole college of physicians could have done nothing in the circumstances. And as the doctor was passed on from tavern to tavern, it was his happy gift to become more silent and secretive. When his wits were going a-woolgathering, he shut up like a Newhaven oyster.

And if vague rumours of evil import were floating in the air, for Grange, as we know, had enemies in abundance, his language and position sufficed to dissipate them. Nothing could be more natural, or in better taste, than the demeanour · of the worthy widower. With ordinary acquaintances, or even with intimates, he betrayed nothing of the sentimental effusiveness which had characterized his letter to Lovat. That had been hastily thrown off in the first paroxysms of distrait and anguish. With calmer reflection the Christian had controlled himself; he accepted the chastening dispensation in a spirit of meekness. He owned freely to faults of temper on his own part, though he insinuated the undeniable provocation. But if he had erred he had been sorely punished, for it would always be borne in upon him, till he stood before the Judgment throne, that things might have been ordered differently had he been more long-suffering and forbearing. "For with all her tantrums and tempers, I loved her well," he would add simply, brushing away a tear from his shaggy eyelashes.

It was a solemn ceremony, the funeral in the Grey Friars. Not a grand funeral by any means, for in the circumstances ostentation would have been an outrage on the *convenances*. But all were bidden to attend who had any title to be there. Though the House of Mar was under a cloud, the near connections of the noble family were numerous, and the lights of the Scottish bar and bench attended, as in duty bound, to show sympathy with their bereaved brother. The unfortunate lady had neither kinsfolk nor friends, and her reputation had been matter of notorious scandal. But she might have filled a great and an honoured place, so all the more did her end seem sad and tragic. There is no service over the grave in the Scotch Church, but Grange's private chaplain offered up the prayer in the lodgings before the coffin was "lifted." The excellent young man prayed with a fervour which impressed the most careless or sceptical of the hearers. For a moment the bereaved husband fairly broke down; he covered his features with his handkerchief, and the mourners averted their eyes from the spectacle of dignity in distress. As the sad procession passed along the streets, preceded by the professionals in their weepers and all the lugubrious livery of woe, the narrow pavements and the close heads were crowded. It was not every day that the good wives of what, after all, was but a small provincial town, had so agreeable a chance of making melancholy holiday. If ejaculations of condolence could have brought comfort to Lord Grange, the sympathy of the populace should certainly have cheered him. Indeed, he was exhilarated and reassured in spite of himself, for he was little used to demonstrations of popularity. And Lovat, who was stalking, Mephistopheles-like, by his side, chuckled in his silent fashion, and nudged the chief mourner with a congratulatory touch of the elbow.

He was soon to be exhilarated in another fashion, nor, indeed, with the manners of the time could he possibly have helped himself. A funeral of respectability meant a debauch, and any funeral of high fashion must be followed by a sumptuous entertain-

ment.   The burial of the Duke of Rothes, when
the procession covered miles of the country roads,
embarrassed a wealthy family for generations; and
at the obsequies of the mother of the Lord President
Forbes, the troops of friends—like Roger of the
" Ingoldsby Legends "—got so excessively drunk,
that they staggered off to the kirkyard, forgetting
the corpse.   In an Edinburgh lodging the company
was necessarily more select, but the guests who went
back from Grey Friars with Grange were none the
less disposed to be convivial and hilarious.   In fact,
they were gathered to discharge a social duty, the
undertaker and the sexton having done with their
tasks.   Those grave senators of the College of Justice,—those devout and sanctimonious divines, had
fortified themselves for the walk to the graveyard
from the glasses and decanters duly handed 'round
at the house.   They came back with sharpened
appetites and suppressed high spirits to the jovial
feast and the serious symposium.

Lovat, who was to face Grange at the table as
croupier, laid a hand on his friend's shoulder as
he followed him up the sombre staircase.

" Ca' canny with the wine, James, and set a

watch on your thirst as well as your lips. You've a
reasonably strong head of your own, but this is the
time to guard it. There's the Advocate, a good friend
of my own, and he could drink either of us under the
table any day. I will not say as much for the agreeable Dromore, though he's a sand bed, like his own
thirsty land by Musselburgh, and there's that cowthy
Armiston lad, with his fine manners and his long
lugs ; mind that he's hand and glove with Walpole
and Islay. It's him that I mistrust the most, for he can
smell out a secret where there is none. And should
he once get wind of this present ploy of ours——"

Grange laid the words of wisdom to heart; he was
moderate, almost to abstemiousness in his potations,
so much so that even the quick-witted Dundas was
inclined to believe in the reality of his sorrow.

Magnum after magnum of the Bordeaux disappeared; bowls of punch followed the wine in
quick succession, still the host set his guests an
indifferent example, and sat silent and absorbed in
spite of their boisterous challenges. Lovat began
to fear his ally was overdoing it, and his comfort was
that the others were so far on, that they would see
little and suspect less. Nevertheless, it was a relief

when Lord Dromore staggered on to his feet, declaring he must be gone to peruse pleadings and draft interlocutors, and, strange to say, such was the strength of custom, probably his lordship took a tolerably clear brain to his business. He was followed by Sir Gilbert Elliot and Armiston, and then the smaller fry of the comforters departed. Lovat fancied he and Grange would be left to a *tête-à-tête*, but Duncan Forbes did not go. It was the more surprising that he was a finished man of the world, punctilious in all social observances, and no intimate of Grange. With Lovat his relations were very different and extremely peculiar. They were near neighbours in the North, and the grey-haired intriguer regarded the younger politician in the light of a friendly though embarrassing guardian. In fact, in the language of the turf, he hedged upon Culloden's friendship and alliance; he had the highest opinion of his sagacity, and he dreaded his instinctive perspicuity. When Lovat was meditating any doubtful affair, his first idea was to put a face upon it to Duncan Forbes. He scarcely hoped that his correspondent would be deceived, but he gave him a plausible brief from which friendship might draw specious pleadings. Moreover, he greatly delighted in his company, but now he scented danger, and could scarcely conceal his uneasiness.

He was not kept in suspense, for Forbes had a purpose, and did not trouble to beat about the bush. The time of the busy Lord Advocate was precious.

"My Lord Grange, perhaps your family owes me little gratitude for the affair of the '15, but I have a good regard for yourself."

Grange bowed somewhat coldly.

"I have a regard for yourself; I have a liking for Simon, though he costs me more anxiety than any dozen other men in Scotland."

"Thanks for the compliment," Lovat broke in. "Here's your health, and long life and more luck to you. We own now you are the master of us all. It's the old story of the child and his mother and the Athenian statesman. I govern the Highlands; you govern me, and how far you are ben with those who govern the British Islands is best known to yourself."

"You will always be jesting, Simon, if you were

F

in the dock or on the scaffold, as you well may be
—and many a time I have told you so—if you do
not heed when a well-wisher gives a word of
warning."

"God forbid!" exclaimed Lovat, with unaffected
indignation, "that I should scorn a hint, to say
nothing of frank speech. I walk through life as
straight as any man, but everywhere are snares
spread for the unwary, and I would never neglect
a kindly warning. So fill up your glass, and
speak out, and be damned to you." The closing of
his broad mouth, the glitter of his steel-grey eyes,
and the involuntary wrinkling of his wide forehead
betrayed an anxiety that belied his words.·

Forbes smiled, and turned to Grange.

"I said I had a regard for yourself and a liking
for Lovat, but beyond that, the Government is
determined to have the country tranquillized. I
break no confidence when I say that that is their
settled policy, and they are resolved to see it
carried out at any cost. There must be no more
unconsidered risings like that which came to an end
at Sheriffmuir. My lord, you are the brother of
the Earl of Mar, and that, let me say, is, in some

ways, a misfortune for you. You are known for a
sound Whig and a good Presbyterian, but blood is
thicker than water, after all, and it is but natural
you should correspond with the banished earl.
May I crave that you will hear me out?" for
Grange made a motion to interrupt.

"I say now, what I could not have said a week
agone, that reports have been flying about in
London to your disadvantage. While your lady
lived it might have been hard to stifle them, if
half of what they said in the South be true. It
was even rumoured you had put your neck under
her petticoat string, and Sir Robert has little
reason to love you."

"I knew not that," broke in Lovat, sarcastically;
—for the life of him, when he had a shaft ready
for his bow, he could not hold his hand; and when
Grange had been returned to Westminster specially
to attack the minister, his maiden speech had been
a signal failure.

"Reason or no," resumed Forbes, "at least, he
had no cause to spare you, and I believe that
the idea was broached in the cabinet that
now was the time to terrorize the waverers by

making some signal example. If they had positive proof—under the writer's hand for example—they would not have hesitated, and it is rumoured that your lady left her home in a huff, and had taken her seat in the stage coach for London. Well' the lady is dead, and her secrets have died with her, and my notion is that all had best be settled peacefully, without further scandal or the shedding of blood. A word suffices for the wise; the King's Advocate asks no questions. A warning has been given if warning were needed; and if I were speaking to plotters or intriguers, I would bid them pass a sponge over the old scores and be good lads for the future. Above all, if I were in their place, I would take a look at my private papers. Nothing more perilous than some scrap of write. I bid you good day, my lords, for the time has flown, but, it may be, it has not been altogether misspent."

*　　*　　*　　*　　*

"What do you say to that, Simon?"

"I say that Forbes is a trusty friend, and that a timely burial may be a blyther business than a wedding. I say that your lordship has been a merciful judge, and I pray that you may never

repent your clemency. And I say farther, that it
shall be my care you do not."

"Draw into the table and fill up your glass;
the folk are gone, and we are free to enjoy ourselves."

CHAPTER VI.

THE ABDUCTION.

WHILE the obsequies of Lady Grange were being celebrated at the Grey Friars, and her husband's friends were drinking to the memory of the departed, her ladyship was very much alive indeed. "She has gone," said the chaplain in his solemn prayer, "where the wicked cease from troubling and the weary are at rest." In sad reality, it was altogether the reverse. The worst of the troubling was still before her, and the rest of the weary was to be indefinitely deferred.

We go back for three eventful days. It was a wild night in early January, the wind from the Firth was howling fiercely round the chimney-pots, and occasionally, in some more violent gust, a shower of sleet and hail was driven against the casements. It was a night when no one would have cared to be abroad, and decent citizens, who generally kept early hours, lay warmly happed up in their blankets. It was the very night when some deed of daring or violence could be ventured with comparative impunity.

Lady Grange's slumbers were not generally so peaceful that she was in any haste to retire. But when the clock in the chamber struck twelve, she took compassion on her waiting-woman and withdrew to her bed-closet. Almost at the moment, as if they had waited for the midnight hour, a party of men entered the darksome close with a sedan chair in their midst. Arrived at the entrance of the common stair leading to Lady Grange's lodging, they stood and whispered; then, taking their orders from one who seemed the chief, they removed their shoes or brogues, for the men were Highlanders, and wore the Highland garb.

Lady Grange, who had only taken off her head-gear, started and listened. It seemed to her that she heard the tread of feet in the room she had just quitted.

"Was the outer door fastened?" she demanded.

"Surely no, my lady. It's never steekit till—"

But the sentence was never finished. The chamber door was thrown open, and the answer

came in the form of half-a-dozen stalwart Highlanders, armed to the teeth.   At a glance the
lady saw that they wore the Fraser tartan, in a
second she saw the hand of Lovat, and was in a
turmoil of self-reproach for her own unpardonable
imprudence.   Why had she not travelled post to
the Border, when she had mortal secrets of desperate men in her keeping?   Oh! why had she not
put herself under sure safeguard, or, at the least,
seen to the surety of her locks and bolts?   But
these reflections came too late, and her attention
was rudely recalled to the immediate circumstances.
Yet the bearing of the man who addressed her
contrasted with his unceremonious entry, and
though he spoke with a pronounced Highland
accent, the manners and speech were those of a
. gentleman of some breeding.

"Your pardon, madam, for forcing ourselves on
your privacy, but we have our orders from those
who maun be obeyed.   On the word of a Highland
gentleman, no harm shall befall you; and if you
will come quietly with us, like a sensible lady, no
incivility shall be offered."

"What would you have with me, men?   Whither

would you take me?" shrieked the unhappy woman, in an agony of apprehension."

" Speer no questions, my lady, for I dare not answer them. It's my counsel to you to keep a quiet sough and let me lead your ladyship down the stairs."

Then the spirit of the daughter of Chiesley burst out; and she broke into a tempest of invective. We may be certain she did not pick her words, but it was the noise and not the abuse that irritated her captor.

" Ten thousand curses on you! will you not be quiet? Well, if you will not, wilful maun have her way."

And stepping forward, he seized her with a strength there was no resisting. As well might the grey hen have struggled in the clutch of the peregrine. Her handkerchief was thrust into her mouth, and firmly secured with her own neckscarf. The ribbon from her waist was knotted round her ankles. Then her ravisher enveloped her in his plaid, and caught her up in his arms as if he had lifted a baby. Not a man had laid finger on anything in the apartment. Meanwhile the foremost of his followers had been doing the same by the bower-maiden. Then a scout having been sent out, who reported that all was safe, the two women were borne down the staircase. The lady was thrust into the sedan chair, where an individual was seated, who clasped her in his arms for the greater security. As for the *suivante*, her ankles were set at liberty, and she was bidden to walk. .The stout Celt who offered her an arm for support, growled a warning into her ear.

"If she skirl or make a sign to the watch or to anybody, de'il tak' me if I dinna drive a dirk to her heart as sune as I wad put my skene-dhu into a roe deer."

The woman took the hint, and tramped forward peaceably enough. Possibly she would have hazarded something in sheer fright had she had any glimmering of the future. Sure it is, that she disappeared somewhere in Lovat's country, and was never heard of again. Any pretence at search subsequently made for the missing woman was directed by those who had safely hidden her away. She may have been married to some rough-handed Fraser, she may have been left to languish in the vaults of Castle Downie, or she may have been casually dropped in some lonely tarn, with a stone to sink her to the bottom. At all events, she passed out of her mistress' story.

And meantime, no trace of that daring irruption was left at the lodging. The door was secured, and the key duly delivered to the honourable gentlemen who had devised the plot and were preparing to carry on the tragic comedy. That no detail or precaution might be overlooked, a sackful of stone and turf was deposited on the chamber floor. For the coffin must be fairly weighted for the funeral, and, as Lovat remarked, facetiously, to his confederate, "You're the less likely to make any miscalculation there, my lord, that they say you can tell the weight of her hand to an ounce."

A wild night it was, and the few folks who were abroad set their faces to the bitter blast and strode doggedly forward. Otherwise any chance wayfarer or civic guardian might well have been surprised to see a group of six or eight riding horses stand shivering on the skirts of the Grassmarket, at the bottom of the Castle Rock.

The men in charge, who were in the secret of

nothing, stamped their feet and swore at large, cursing the delays that kept them on duty. The flying snow drift had whitened the steeds till, as they stood with drooping crests and tails tucked in, they looked like so many statues in marble.

" Puir beasts! " said one compassionate groom.

" Puir beasts, indeed! " exclaimed a less merciful comrade. " If I'm not the more mistook, they'll be hot enough before many hours are gone by. I've a mind to hand ye over the bundle o' bridles and slip ower the way to Luckie McGill's for a mutchkin."

" For God's sake, Duncan, beware what you do! I take to the Glenlivet as kindly as any man, but if auld Simon has his crooked fingers in this pie, as I well believe, he'll give us our kail through the reek if we fail him. Then it's hell-brose in place of usquebagh ye'd be supping, I'm thinking. But, hark!—what's that I hear; aye, it is—I hear the whustle."

He whistled himself, low, but shrill, and sharp came the response. A squall tore the black clouds asunder; the dark silhouette of the Castle battlements stood out clear, high over head, against a strip of sky gemmed over with stars, and a pale moon, wading through a fringe of watery haze, cast fitful lights on the scene enacting below. The little train with the sedan chair came to a halt. The horses were stripped of their snowy wrappings, and a man, mounting a strong flea-bitten grey garron, said : " Lift her out, my lads, and be brisk, and hand her up behind me."

In these days the pillion was a common means of conveyance, and often had Lady Grange ridden in that fashion behind her lord or some other cavalier to kirk or to merry-making. But never had she dreamed of such a ride as this—in such circumstances, at such an hour, or in such weather. The gag was still there, though loosened, so as to give her more freedom of breathing. The plaid was removed from her head, so that she could look about her, but it still swathed her arms to her sides, and the tight bandage that secured her feet was pricking them with thousands of pins and needles. Helpless as she was, fear of falling there was none, for she was so tightly buckled to the horseman before her by a hair-girth that she could feel each heave of his chest.

She might have bowed herself to ask for pity—
who knows! she might have promised silence and
acquiescence in exchange for a little liberty. But
the anguish of it was that she had neither the choice
nor the opportunity. What passed at that time
through that reeling brain, through that convulsed
body, irresistibly coerced and constrained, none can
guess or realize. What the human frame can
endure, so frail in some respects, yet so tenacious
of its vitality, is one of the inscrutable mysteries of
physiology. A touch on a brain nerve may make a
raving maniac, a clot of blood in an artery may mean
sudden death, and yet men have drifted for days in
an open boat in the tropics, surviving the tortures
of thirst and famine ; and women have been disen-
tombed alive from the cells of the Inquisition after
years of torture, bodily and mental. So that Lady
Grange should have lived through the first stage of
that ride, is rather a proof of human vitality than
a phenomenon. But seldom can such intensity of
suffering have been comprised within so brief a space.
It may have been that she was saved by the mental
anguish reacting like an anodyne on the bodily
pain. It is certain that, as she told her story

afterwards—and in the circumstances it is almost incredible that she could have exaggerated—her brain had never been more active, her sensibilities never more acute. She had marked and remembered the slightest incident, and the sights that passed before her were as fuel to the fire. She felt from the first that her fate was sealed, though what it might be was in a horror of obscurity. Her angry passion turned upon herself, like the fire-encompassed scorpion, stinging itself in impotent fury—as again she cursed the reckless imprudence which had left her to the mercy of men who could never forgive. Had she known that they meant to make away with her, it would have been an immediate relief, although life was sweet and vengeance sweeter. But it was clear they had no immediate murder in their minds, and she shuddered with the fear and the cold, as she conjured up the lingering torture they might reserve for her.

How she was now; what she had been; and what she might have been. Another rift in the clouds, another bright blink of the moonshine. Yes, there was the dark outline of the old house of Kirkliston on the side of Corstorphine Hill, where

she had gone in the gaiety of girlhood to her first
dance, and walked her first minuet with the bril-
liant James Erskine. How well she remembered
the throbbing of her heart when he snatched the
blush-rose from her bodice. And the nook into
which the lover had withdrawn her, where kisses
had followed the theft of the flower, for it was love
at first sight, and a love-match with burning passion on both sides. Memory flashed back to the
anticipated joys of the honeymoon; when the spell
of her charms had held him so fast, that he had
fulfilled the pledges given in moments of passion.
Would that he had never played her false. She
would have been a loving wife, as she told herself, had he been a faithful husband; she would
never have given place to the devil, or yielded
to the follies or vices which condemned her in
the eyes of the world. It was too late for re-
grets or even for repentance; had she been wiser
and more womanly, things might have been
otherwise, but, after all, was it not her tyrant
who should bear the blame? The softer flow of
the fond old memories was swamped in a gush
of the waters of bitterness, and she vowed she

would live to be revenged, if strength of will could do it.

The party halted at a wayside change house, to break their fast and rest their horses. The captive sat sullenly by the corner of the fire, till, with a thousand pains shooting through the bones and nerves, her cramped and frozen limbs were unchilled. Absorbed and abstracted, she scarcely felt the pain. But, to the surprise of those who had rather hoped to tame her by hunger, she ate of the coarse fare, and drank of the milk they offered. They laughed when she asked for the whisky bottle, and dashed the strong spirit into the milk cup. But the woman had sworn to live, and she knew the restorative that suited her.

CHAPTER VII.

CAGED.

It was grey dawn when they drew bridle at the gates of the old mansion house of Wester Polmaise. Forewarned that she was approaching her temporary place of abode, she roused herself to brush the hoar-frost from her eyes and look out with keen, curious anxiety. Nothing could be more forbidding, chilly, and cheerless than the prospect in this immediate foreground of the dim and terrible future. Her spirit sunk at the aspect of the grim feudal tower approached by a short avenue of battered ash trees, crowded together in places elsewhere with ugly gaps, and throwing out against the grey heavens the skeleton arms that seemed to be racked and gnarled by the rheumatism that prematurely crippled the farm folk. There were narrow windows, distributed regardless of plan; there was a battlement, and there were bartizans in the style of the sixteenth century, when a man's nearest neighbour might be his deadly foe; the high-pitched roof, of more recent date, rose on the ridges in a succession of "crow's feet;" the slates were covered with a thick growth of stone-crop where the wind had swept away the snow, and the only sign of life about the place was a thin thread of smoke curling up from one of the chimneys. As for the outbuildings, with the great rifts in the thatch and the broken rafters, they scarcely offered shelter for the overridden cattle. And the dreary picture was completed by an unsavoury dung-heap, on which starveling fowls were scraping and pecking, and by the jackdaws, whose clamour was stilled by the cold, and who sat on the roof-tree observant, hunched up in so many ruffled balls of feathers.

Once the traces of the prisoner were lost, the Bastille itself could not be a safer place of keeping, and so the lady thought.

> " A merry house, mayhap, in days of yore,
>   But something ailed it now.
>   The place was cursed—"

And surely to be shunned by all and sundry. At the stamping of hoofs on the flags and the loud oaths of the riders, the iron-clinched door in the low archway was opened by a bare-armed and bare-legged servant girl, staring stupidly. She was the *demoiselle de château*, and apparently the sole occupant. She had expected the arrival, but seemed to have made no preparation. The man who had ridden before Lady Grange lifted her down and carried her into the house, for she was incapable of walking. The entrance hall struck cold and damp as a funeral vault. What a change from the well-warmed rooms of Preston, with the roaring sea-coal fires, the glistening panelling, the tapestries, and the pictures! Here everything was of bare stone. The massive walls were trickling with wet. The foot splashed in collected puddles. The winding staircase, with its broken steps, was dimly lighted by slits and loopholes, and yet when she was borne into the apartment assigned for her use, the mockery of furnishing made desolation more desolate. There was a huge four-posted bed, with tattered hangings in one corner, looking like a hearse that had done its work and been laid up in ordinary: there were a rickety table and a chair or two with moth-eaten coverings. For hangings there were spider's webs in abundance, and the windows, set in walls four feet in thickness, were begrimed with filth where the panes had not been replaced with rags. Some shreds of tattered matting were spread on the floor, mildewed with damp and smelling abominably, for the window sashes refused to open.

The most passionately emotional spirits are the most sensitive to their surroundings. In the free air, as she proved afterwards, however hard her fate, Lady Grange would have speedily regained courage and resolution. She would have braced herself to surmount her difficulties and stimulated energy by effort. But in this loathsome dungeon, in this *oubliette* into which she had been dropped, she collapsed in the depths of depression. Happily for her, perhaps, her indomitable vitality was paralysed for the time, and her benumbed faculties lost much of the consciousness of suffering. She sat staring helplessly stupefied into the fire, which would not burn up, while the atmosphere was made fouler by the fumes of the smoke, for the chimney was half-choked by the nests of the jackdaws. Through that long day she refused to eat, and, indeed, the food was hardly likely to tempt her. The first sign of life she gave was when she asked at early nightfall for her waiting-woman. The answer was that the woman was gone, and that she must be content to wait upon herself or to put up with male attendance. She scarcely seemed to heed; in the blackness of despair, a trouble more or less did not matter. She sat on stupidly, with her brain a blank, by the light of the smoking lamp that barely lighted up the table.

Then came the inevitable stinging revulsion. She woke up as one wakens in a hideous dream, or as a patient emerges from the influence of an anæsthetic to the pains and after-sensations of some horrible operation. But the waking thoughts were worse than any nightmare, and the brain suddenly became terribly clear. The numb paralysis somewhat restored her, and now she had power and strength to think. The excitement of the rape and the miseries of the road were no longer present to excite or preoccupy. The day had gone by comparatively well, but it would be idle to try to depict the sufferings of the interminable night. Now she would pace her chamber like a caged tiger-cat, with wild gesticulations and moans and pitiful lamentations mingled with furious maledictions. The Highlander told off to lie outside her door, though little given to sentiment or the melting mood, would cross himself and shiver with superstitious dread before turning over to try to sleep again. Then her temper would change ; she would throw herself on the bed, and with a violent effort of that will on which she prided herself, try to forget her sorrows in slumber and husband her strength for the day of vengeance. Sleep she could not, but there she lay, indifferent to the rats that squeaked behind the panelling, that chased each other across her pillows, and fought and worried over the supper she had left untouched on the table.

The longest night comes to an end at last, but if there be an hour of deadly depression to the sick or suffering, it is when darkness disappears and the day is breaking. The night is shaking off her cerements, and all creation seems to shiver. Lady Grange rose and tottered across the room; she tore out a bundle of clouts from one of the windows. The rush of biting air refreshed her body, but it struck cold to her heart. She looked out on a terraced garden given over to neglect, that might be beautiful in its untrimmed luxuriance in the summer-time, with the sweet briar, the half-wild honeysuckle, and the bourtree bushes. She looked beyond over the frosted fallows and the grey stone dykes, to the low hills skirting the northern horizon, where the snows were melting into the snow-laden clouds. A cold, grey mist hung heavily in the hollows; a hare was limping along as if a night in his form had crippled him; a flock of starlings and troops of sparrows were chattering or twittering as in impatient complaint. The lad leading a raw-boned horse to the watering was beating his arms and blowing in his fingers. None of them seemed very happy, yet how she envied them all. What would she not have given for the wings of those starlings, or for the un-fettered legs of that lumbering hobbledehoy! But after all, neither birds nor boy had a purpose, and there she felt the superiority of a being with a soul, and comforted herself with her capacity for vindictive endurance. The sharper the suffering, the nobler the power of endurance, and the sweeter the assurance of revenge, however long it might be waited for. Bargains with the powers of darkness in the Middle Ages, according to all legend and tradition, were matters of everyday occurence. They were supposed to have gone out of date in Scotland towards the beginning of the eighteenth century. But if ever a woman was willing to sell herself to Satan it was Lady Grange, when she prayed that morning rather to the devil than to God, that she might be spared to see her desire upon her enemies.

The days dragged on to weary weeks, and she became dully, sullenly settled in her habits. She lived a life of silence and solitude. The single female domestic had nothing to say when she chanced to meet her. If the woman was not half-witted, she simulated something like idiocy. Most of the party who had carried her off were gone, but three men remained. One, who seemed to order the others about, and who appeared of somewhat superior station, answered her curtly when addressed, but avoided all conversation. The other two, although they wore the Lowland dress, were Highlandmen, and "had little English." They were not uncivil, although roughly unsympathetic. It was they who did all the waiting. They brought her meals, they swept out her chambers; from time to time they even made her bed, when she did not spare them the trouble. Soon she ceased to have any delicacy in the matter, regarding them rather as animated statues than as beings of flesh and blood. The door of her chamber was kept locked, but she was permitted to take exercise when it pleased her. To be sure, she was always under the eyes of a sentry when she stirred abroad, and her walks were limited to the little garden. When she paced the weed-grown paths on the terrace, broken down by earth-slips and land-springs, the watchman never for a moment lost sight of her. At first she had rebelled against the perpetual constraint—against the living manacles in which she moved. She confined herself to her room; she refused to touch her food till absolutely compelled by the pangs of hunger; her sole pleasure was in looking forward to the visit of her gaoler, when she overwhelmed him with a storm of invective which brought temporary relief. She soon discovered that the stolid man-in-waiting cared as little for abuse as for the pelting of a summer shower; indeed, although he had more English than he professed at first, he understood very little of her bitter objurgation.

She felt her bodily strength was failing, and, moreover, she knew that her spirits were being tamed by the deprivation of the stimulants that had become a necessity. Then this woman of iron will, though violent passion, changed her tactics, and pulled herself together, before the power of resolution had altogether gone. She demanded an interview with her head-keeper, complained of illness, and asked to see a doctor. For a moment he hesitated; perhaps he felt he would best fulfil the wishes of his employers by letting dangerous illness run its course. But, after all, he was not paid to be an accomplice in a murder, and possibly he was moved by compassion, for the captive, though past her prime, was still fair to look upon, and could throw something of her old fascination into her eyes when she chose. He demurred to the doctor; said his orders were peremptory as to intercourse with the outer world; but added that, within the measure of his ability, he would do all in his power to pleasure her ladyship.

The upshot was that he undertook to furnish the medical prescriptions she specially desired. Thenceforth there was no lack of tolerable wine, nor did the lady disdain the occasional bottle of whisky, which her Highland guards regarded as the real elixir of life. The coarse but wholesome fare became palatable. She forced herself to eat; then the eating ceased to be an effort, and became a resource and relaxation to which she looked forward. She got her nerves generally under control, relieving them with occasional paroxysms of temper, when, believing herself out of sight and earshot, she heaped execrations on the heads of Grange and Lovat which would have made their blood run cold, had they been still at her mercy. That one day they would be at her mercy was the hope which ever sustained her. And her husband would have been more anxious than he was; possibly he might have been driven to more desperate courses, had she not had the courage to keep her counsel, and apparently to acquiesce in her fate.

CHAPTER VIII.

CAPTIVE AND GAOLER.

IT was so far satisfactory to the conspiring gossips in Edinburgh to learn that the lady had turned wise and purpose-like, and was like to give little further trouble. "At first," reported her guardian, "she would beat herself about, like a new-caught gled against the bars of her cage, but now, for the most part, she is conformable as a brooding fowl."

Nevertheless, they had their reasons for anxiety, or rather Grange had, for the grave ex-Lord of Justiciary had still some character to lose, whereas if Lovat had been charged without being convicted of playing the leading part in the abduction, and having arranged the grim comedy of the mock funeral by way of throwing the hounds of the law off his trail, he would have been inclined to consider it all as another feather in his cap.

Ugly rumours were flying about; whispers and

suspicious looks began to inspire sinister forebodings, Lovat was in the way of walking up and down like Satan; he was here to-day and gone to-morrow; he had a safe retreat at Castle Downie, or he might cross the seas at the worst, if the Government seemed like to give him trouble. Grange had his mansion, his ties, and his station in Edinburgh; he knew well that he was always watched by deadly enemies; and if he were brought to the bar of the Court in which he had presided, whether the verdict were "guilty," or "not proven," he would be ruined, beggared, and virtually outlawed. The disappearance of his wife's waiting-woman had become an embarassing feature in the case. It had been given out, by the counsel of Lovat, that the woman had disappeared with valuable jewels, and a warrant was duly obtained for her apprehension.

So far, so well. Even if the officers were foolish enough to be over-zealous, the woman was so effectually hidden away that there was no chance of finding her. If they did hit on one end of the clue, there would be no following it up, and suspicions are far removed from proof. But the latest news from West Lothian were more serious.

The custodian of the prisoner, though satisfied as
to her behaviour, had begun to get uneasy about
himself and his charge. It was a peaceful neigh-
bourhood with little stirring, yet the people were
beginning to talk. The old wives, and the men,
too, for that matter, would make the most of a
mystery when they had once gotten wind of one;
some queer story might make itself wings, and be
wafted even as far as Edinburgh. It was for their
lordships to judge; but now he had told them
his mind, he would do his duty as before, and
leave their lordships to take care of the consequences.

"All things considered," said Lovat, one night,
"the sooner she's shifted and settled the better.
You know yourself, James, that if you're in trouble
there's nobody but yourself to blame. Had I
had my way, and had it not been for your tender
fancies, she would have been travelling to the
North, winter or no winter."

"She would have been smothered in the snow
drifts of Brander or Glencoe, or swallowed in the
waters of some flooded ford."

"Maybe," said Lovat, coolly, "and maybe no.

Anyhow in place of trusting her to the care of Providence, you were so dooms particular that you would be her Providence yourself. But now that the winter is drawing on to the spring, for both our sakes she's bound to be moving. And I care not if I start her on her travels myself. I have business with Kilmarnock at Callander. As well a hand off as a finger, aye, wagging. I can take Wester Polmaise on my way. So I'll be drawing on my riding-boots with the morrow's dawn, and the Lord Simon of Lovat would be scarce likely to take the road without a sufficient attendance on foot and on horseback."

"Faith, Simon, I know no man of your rank who rides as a rule with fewer followers. Like the hill fox in the bracken, the less that's seen of you, for the most part, the better you're pleased. The fashions you picked up among the Jesuits and the go-betweens of St. Germains serve ye right well, and have saved you many a time."

"That's sure enough, my lord, but circumstances alter cases. It sets us both now that there should be no semblance of concealment; moreover, I want men and need a reason for taking them. I shall give your lady fair convoy to the Brig of Stirling where it is possible that the garrison folks might be fashious with honest travellers. At Stirling I bid her God speed and take my leave, and turn back to seek my night's quarters at the house of Callander. I have affairs of import to talk over with my lord."

Next day there was unwonted excitement in the grass-grown courtyard before the old West Lothian mansion. Within there was hurrying to and fro: without there was such a gallant train as the old house had not seen for many a day. Lady Grange, in natural excitement, rushed to a window. A tall and dignified old gentleman, in warm boot hose, and wrapped in a richly furred cloak, was dismounting from a splashed and jaded steed: the castellan who acted seneschal to her was obsequiously holding his stirrup. The rider, laying a hand on the man's shoulder, swung himself heavily to the ground, swore a hearty oath, and stamped his half-frozen feet. With the impatience of chafing age and the habit of bullying command over humble dependants, Lovat cut short the other's courtesies.

"A truce to ceremony, man, and tell me this—
you got my message?"

"Aye, and I am at your lordship's commands—"

"Well, and what my lordship commands is this
—food and fire, fire and food. The wine and strong
waters I've brought myself : I could not trust that
to your tasting."

The table was soon spread, and his lordship
dined fully and drank freely. As he dined and
drank he thawed, in the company of two or three of
his attendants, who all wore the hawk's feather in
their bonnets, and called themselves Duihnewassels.
They all laughed at his jests, and one of the parasites, at least, had wit enough to flatter his tyrant's
vanity. What with the warmth, the food, the
liquor, and the joviality, Lovat got into the most
genial of his moods. He looked forward in the
way of dessert to a voluptuous indulgence in his
natural cruelty. He meant to play with the
prisoner as a cat with a mouse, before finally
pronouncing her doom and closing the doors of
hope. He hated her as much as it was in his cold
nature to hate anybody, for she was not one of the
stumbling-blocks in his path which he could simply

curse and kick aside. Moreover, she took unfair
licence with the privileges of her sex, in refusing
either to be cajoled or coerced. Besides all that, he
blamed her for her husband's obstinacy; for had
Grange only looked at things from a rational point
of view, she might have been really resting in
peace at the Greyfriars, instead of troubling him
at Polmaise. So he smiled complacently, and
metaphorically licked his lips, when he gravely
charged her keeper with the respectful message
that Lord Lovat would be honoured in waiting
upon the Lady Grange at her ladyship's convenience.

Her ladyship had been anxiously awaiting the
interview, although she had not expected that it
would be announced with ceremonious formality,
and she was somewhat taken aback. She was
carried away from the dark present to the days
when she had been a free woman—free as Lovat
himself, to indulge her caprices and fancies.
Hopes were excited which she strove to repress,
for reason told her they must prove delusive. Her
enemies were too deeply committed to draw back.
Yet already she had summoned all her self-control

to take advantage of her last opportunity. She remembered she was playing her last stroke, and she surmised all that might befall her if she lost. It was for life or living death—for liberty or lingering despair. If she lost, there was really nothing left but vengeance. Perhaps, too, her fiery spirit had been somewhat tamed by solitude, anxiety, and suffering. She hated Lovat far more than he hated her: but better make a bargain and come to a compromise than close finally with his master, Satan, and sell herself irredeemably to the Enemy.

Lovat had climbed the stairs with unsteady feet, but a cool head, prepared to throw himself into the play, as an actor confident of his genius for improvisation. The scene would be stormy, but he was sure of his crushing success in the *dénouement*. He was prepared for tears and prayers, for expostulations, execrations, and all the frenzies of a maddened Medea. Then he would deal with her as the calm physician with the lunatic, pronounce the words of doom, and leave his victim to her reflections. He thought of Lady Grange as an elderly vixen, aged by her passions and prematurely faded by sensual indulgences. Lovat was a

professed connoisseur in female beauty, and he was
surprised and perhaps softened by what he saw.
There was no termagant to receive him, careless of
her toilette and violent in speech. What he saw
was a lady, certainly past her prime, but still
retaining more than the traces of no ordinary
beauty. Perhaps the enforced quiet and temperate
living had embellished her, but sure it was that
she seemed to have renewed her youth, and he
could understand how she had still some hold on
her husband. He had prepared himself for a
storm of abuse, but she did the honours of the
wretched room with a graceful and touching
courtesy. Lovat, though always a villain, and a
barbarian to boot in his northern domains, was
still outwardly a gentleman in the South. He
could not choose but answer Lady Grange with
the same courtesy with which she addressed
him. And the generous Bordeaux had disposed
him to good humour. It appeared as if this
schemer of iron resolution might be won to
her wishes. She pleaded with him tearfully and
pathetically. She dwelt in touching language
on her wrongs : she frankly owned that her

wifely jealousy had driven her to rash and desperate extremities.

"I tell you honestly, my good lord, that I bore you a grievous grudge for having been the cause and the prime agent in my captivity. Now, as God is my witness, I not only forgive you, but am grateful. For this weary seclusion has restored me to a better mind, and I have exorcised the demon of jealousy that possessed me. Take me back to the world from which you have taken me, and believe in my eternal and devoted gratitude. For your sake—for the sake of my friend and benefactor—for the future I shall be the most submissive of wives. Ask of me any guarantees and they shall be given; only intercede for me with Lord Grange, and carry me back in honour to my lodgings."

She sunk on her knees, seized the long bony hand of Lovat, and pressed her burning lips upon it. Was she in earnest or was she acting a part? Probably at the moment, in her passion for liberty, as she would pledge herself to anything, she believed she would keep her pledges. Probably Lovat hesitated, and might even have yielded. The vanity of the old *roué* was pleasantly tickled. There was a touch of tenderness in the lady's voice, there was a wistful look in the lustrous grey eyes, which made him fancy he could reclaim the wild haggard to his whistle, and hold her by the jesses of her heart-strings. For as there is no fool like an old fool, so no one is so easily hoodwinked on occasion as one who holds women in supreme contempt. He was so much moved that he forgot the false polish of his manner, and with a low, doubtful whistle turned to look out of the window. But from his subtle familiar came a sudden prompting. He turned with startling swiftness upon the kneeling petitioner. He caught the gleam of hopeful triumph in her eyes, and saw the snare into which he had so nearly fallen. Each understood the other, and deception was at an end. Had he doubted, he must have been convinced by the passionate vin-dictiveness, the concentrated malignity of those flashing eyes. For all the softness had vanished, and her unexpected approach to success had re-animated the slumbering spirit of vengeance.

The revulsion with Lovat was at least as strong. He realized that he had been lured to the brink of a precipice: and the vanity which had been agreeably flattered was now as bitterly mortified. Moreover, if this elderly Circe had so nearly befooled him, she might be more dangerous than he could have believed with impressionable youth. Happily his eyes had been opened in time, and he had his crushing retort in readiness. He had only to stick to his original resolutions. The changed situation was so clear, that he did not trouble about preliminaries.

"I may say what I am here to say, very shortly. Your husband, who is still more uxorious than his friends would wish him, is willing to spare you the shame of a public scandal. He has stretched a point and passed sentence in private, and in his infinite mercy and goodness has determined you shall have space and time for repentance. The remaining term of your life, be it long or short, will be passed in solitude, beyond the sounds of our southern speech. May the Lord grant you the grace to turn yourself to prayers and penitence."

"Simon Fraser, you are a pre-doomed and God-forsaken hypocrite. I may yet be spared to make you suffer in this life; but miserable as I am, I would be more miserable still, were I not as sure as you are standing there of the certainty of eternal vengeance. I see you now in the hottest nook of hell-fire, and you, who have been a bibber of wine, shrieking out for a cup of cold water."

Lovat was rather amused than otherwise. The impotent writhing of the victim he held in his hand had already taken off the edge of his anger. He answered lightly, with another turn of the screw.

" I pity you too much, poor woman, to mind your flyting or your miscalling me. For your sins you are doomed to dree your weird, and a dismal weird it is like to be. There is something of the second sight said to run in my line, and I can see a weeping and wailing woman, waiting for the hour that maybe is to bring her relief, and shut up in the prison walls of grey rock and green water. Her lullaby, when she lies down on a foul-smelling pillow of fulmar down, is the roar of the surge and the skirl of the seafowl. But there or elsewhere, what does it matter? There can be small mirth in the music when the devil is piping to his own."

"And so you possess the second sight, Simon Fraser. Well, for all I can tell, you may have it, you double-squinting fiend. But do not think that you alone can foresee the future, you may doubtless dispose to your pleasure. I can see farther, and now I have clearer vision than ever St. John saw in the Apocalypse."

She tossed back her grey streaked tresses with both hands, and stared him in the face with mystical significance.

" I see the old grizzled wolf hunted down at last, in spite of all his wiles and his windings. I see a hoary hypocrite, standing at the bar, and his grey head brought to the traitor's block, with the contempt of all honest folk, and the flyting of the very dregs of the people. It is the Calvary of a Barabbas, and the villain's ignominy shall be handed down to all time in history, so that he shall be the shame of his ancient line. My eternal curse cling to you, Simon : in life or in death, in bed or at board, may the memory of this meeting and parting abide with you. Aye, if looks could kill, you would kill me now, but I know well that your power is limited, and does not extend to immediate murder. Whether God or my husband holds you back, I know not. But remember this, and take the message to James Erskine, that the sword is hanging by a hair over both your heads. I curse you both, not with the

merciful threat of speedy death, but with the
assurance of anxiety that will never be appeased
save when you drown it with the wine, and then God
help you on your waking in the morning. Now,
good my lord, you have my leave to go."

CHAPTER IX.

THE JOURNEY.

LOVAT, like all Highlanders, was superstitious.
The interview had ended very differently from
what he had anticipated ; it had given him matter
for grave reflection, and perhaps for the time he
suffered almost as keenly as the lady. The first
sign of his discomfiture was an abrupt change of
plan : instead of giving her a convoy in person
over Stirling Bridge, he decided to ride forward
and leave her to follow under guard, even at
greater risk of detection. For the moment the
schemer had half lost his head, heated as it was
with wine and anger, and he was thinking less of
the present than of the future. The few attendants he took with him knew the mood, and did
not dare to intrude on his gloomy meditations.
The words of burning passion were still ringing
in his ears, nor could he shake off the sinister
impression that the curses might work out to ful-

filment. Men said of him that notwithstanding his affectation of piety, he neither feared God nor regarded man; but there they were not altogether right. There were times when the former convert of the Jesuits felt slavish terror of a God of vengeance, although he never thought of turning in penitence to a God of love. He felt and acted like one who, having sold himself to Satan, could only assure the support of his master by recourse to Satanic devices. Some day, perhaps, he might square accounts with heaven, but there was pressing business to be attended to in the meantime. At that moment Lady Grange's life hung on a thread. The solemn oath to Erskine never weighed with him, but there were more practical considerations.

"The fool might have what he calls searchings of heart, and in some such paroxysm of remorse he would not hesitate to sacrifice me. The oath and evidence of the brother of Mar, and a former Lord of Justiciary, would be ill to get over, even if it did not establish legal presumption of guilt. Nothing should be more natural than a mishap in the pass of Glencoe or in the hills of Lochaber.

This is a season when the rivers are always in speat, and the bridle paths broken down on the face of the precipices. But putting James Erskine out of account, there is the reckoning with MacLeod and MacDonald. Those Western Highlanders stand kittle on their honour when they have little to fear, and, judging other men like themselves, would be ready to mistrust their own fathers. If the woman came to an ill end by the blessing of Providence, the devil would not persuade them that I was not at the bottom of the business, and when once whispers of the kind are in the air, they go drifting through the country like thistledown. If the irons in the fire are not to scorch my fingers,—if I cannot spare my conscience,—I must endeavour to keep my character."

So, having made up his mind that matters in the meanwhile must be left to drift, he tightened his bridle, drove the spurs into his steed, changed the current of his thoughts by a sharp canter on the level, and then, calling a trusted follower to his side, began to discuss the political schemes which he meant to be the subject of the evening's conversation.

* * * * *

A second and smaller cavalcade, with the captive in charge, followed at a somewhat more leisurely pace. While the road still lay through the Lowlands, it was a delicate affair to avoid awkward challenges and accidental encounters. They passed boroughs in the charge of well-affected magistrates, and houses in the possession of men who might have willingly come to the rescue. Stirling was held by a strong garrison, and the adjacent country was patrolled by occasional detachments. Fortunately for the venture of the ravishers, the season was in their favour. It was only natural that a woman riding on a pillion should be secured and well protected against the nipping cold. Lady Grange was wrapped up in mantles, and her head was hooded so as to hide the gag applied like a tight-fitting respirator. It gave her barely freedom to breathe, and articulate speech was impossible. She was mounted on a stout hackney behind Alexander Foster, of Carsbonny, who headed the party, and was made responsible for her safe delivery at her destination. Foster, though a careless adventurer, was neither cruel nor ill-natured; nor was he altogether insensible to close contact with a woman who had still the power to fascinate. He knew besides that if he dared there was a double game to play; and that if he brought her into relations with the Ministers of the Crown he might be richly rewarded for a piece of good service. But Lovat had him in his power, and could certainly hang him unless treachery secured his indemnity as part of the reward. Moreover, he knew his master, as his master knew him. Behind him rode Peter Fraser, lithe, active, and keen-eyed as a Highland deer-hound, whose hand was ever travelling instinctively to his pistol or his dirk—*ame damnée*, in a subaltern capacity of the chieftain. And he shrewdly suspected, doubtless with truth, that Peter had instructions to dispose of him on the slightest symptom of treachery.

But who can describe the feelings of the prisoner as she saw opportunity after opportunity slipping by, and realized that with succour often within arm's reach she was nevertheless being lost beyond redemption. If her husband was living under the sword of Damocles, she was submitting then to the torments of Tantalus. She felt like

the seeming corpse in a trance of suspended
animation, about to be screwed down in the coffin
and consigned to the tomb. It was a marvel that
no vessel burst in the brain, when the blood was
surging in her aching head, and the pulses were
throbbing as if they would have burst her temples.
But memory and sensation were morbidly acute,
as when she had been carried on that morning
from Edinburgh to Polmaise.

She never was nearer a stroke of apoplexy, or
suffocation from intense emotion, than in the little
wayside hostelry of the Torwood. The party had
pulled up, late in the afternoon, to bait the horses
and to refresh themselves. Foster had lifted her from
the horse, and led her into the little kitchen. The
smoke from the peat on the open hearth swirled
between the earthern floor and the blackened rafters.
He had placed her with a certain courtesy on the
settle, and having given his orders as to unpacking
the provision basket they had brought with them,
was about to remove the mufflings and the gag.
The clatter of hoofs approaching at a rapid pace
made him change his purpose. A jovial voice was
heard without, and then a gentleman, stooping his

I

head, stumbled in at the low doorway, and stood blinking like an owl in the sunshine in the darksome den. The peat smoke filled his eyes with water, and he could distinguish little. He was a square-shouldered Hercules, with a frank and jovial face, but a certain swagger of manner, which marked him as one likely to quarrel on slight provocation. He had pistols in his belt and a long rapier by his side, and behind him were a couple of stalwart serving men. He could distinguish nothing save the shrouded female in the corner, but the lady knew him well. Had she searched Scotland from Cape Wrath to the Border, she could scarcely have happened upon a more hopeful champion. It was Livingstone, of Carron, who was known far and wide for a fearless dare-devil, and famous for more than one bloody duel; she had met him often at dance or revel, and there had been sundry passages of flirtation between them. She flattered herself, besides, that tender remembrances might have something to do with the virulence with which he spoke habitually of her husband, whom he cursed for a traitor and sanctimonious hypocrite. For hate of him, or love of

her, or for pure devilry, he would have gone far to
do Grange an evil turn. His hereditary mansion
house looked down on the Crooks of Forth, and the
Carse of Stirling was full of his friends and kinsfolk.
A word or a sign, and the Quixotic champion of
dames would have followed up the adventure, all
the rather if there were to be speedy pistol shots
and the clashing of swords. But her features were
shrouded, her lips were sealed, and even her arms
were belted to her sides.

Foster failed to realize all the danger, but he
was on his guard, and equal to the occasion. As
Livingstone stood rubbing his eyes and curiously
regarding the silent female, the other accosted him
and named himself.

"Aye, I have heard of you before, though I have
never had the fortune to fall in with you," said
Livingstone. "A henchman of Lord Simon's, and
I see the Fraser tartan. Nay, no offence, man;
I speak in all good faith, and it is no time for
friends to be falling out. But is the old fox at the
old game of carrying off the prey to his earths in
Strath Beauly?"

Even had he not made the secret Jacobite sign,

raising his hand to his drooping Spanish hat, it was not Foster's cue to quarrel.

For the moment, the situation was critical. Livingstone had turned towards him, and had his back towards Lady Grange. Fettered as she was, her legs were free, and she was stretching out a foot to attract the new comer's attention. She was doomed to banishment to an immeasurable distance from all that made life worth living; once beyond the abyss that severed civilization from Celtic barbarism, and the gates of hope would be irrevocably closed, and now there was but a bare inch between her and certain rescue. By a happy excess of precaution, though partly in the apprehension she might swoon and fall, Foster had strapped her to the settle. If Livingstone made the slightest backward movement—if the captive, choking in her agony, made a noise or a sign, the plot was exploded, and he was compromised with his master, as slow to forgive a blunder as a fault. But Foster, like Lovat, had been a *habitué* of St. Germains: he had not only presence of mind, but the ready plausibility of a secret agent. He answered with an air of frank good-fellowship, at the same time responding to the sign, and touching his lips with his finger.

"The less reason to fall out, that I must pray you to keep my secret. I'm on my lord's business, as you suppose, and as it craves both speed and urgency, maybe he would be none the better pleased if he knew that I were giving a far-away cousin a convoy on the road to Crieff. Goat's milk and loch trout, and the air of the hills—its all I can help her to, and you would not have me grudge it."

"D—n the goat's milk, but you need have made no mention of the trout, for I doubt I'll find nothing so savoury in this cursed smoky hole. Bannocks and a brandered brood hen, at the best of it."

"When things seem at the worst, they're like to mend," said Foster, falling in with his humour. "I was just unpacking the fare to set forth a table in the wilderness ; we will have it laid out there on that bonny green bank in the caller air, and maybe you will do us the honour to share the cheer."

"Will I not, man ; and the rather that you may give me some speerings of our friends over the water."

And bringing his hand down on the other's

shoulder with a force that made him wince, he
strode out of the cabin. Thenceforth the two were
sworn brothers, and the rude meal was washed
down with draughts of wine and caulkers of
usquebagh. And still the lady sat within, listen-
ing to the obstreperous mirth that mocked her
misery.

The haphazard boon companions took effusive
leave of each other, when they sounded reluctantly
again to boot and saddle. Reluctantly, at least, on
Livingstone's part, for Foster was glad enough to
get rid of his unwelcome guest. But the embarrassing interview came as a timely warning. Thence-
forward he would keep to cover through the day,
and travel only in the darkness. A strange state
of the troubled country where, from fear or
kindness, he was assured at any stage of secure
harbourage, with no inconvenient questioning.
And a stronger tribute to the ascendancy of the
Scottish Machiavelli, who had spun his cobwebs
over the breadth of the land was that men of all
conditions were caught and entangled in them.

There was no trouble at the dreaded Brig of
Stirling. The little cavalcade passed it in the

silence of the night, with no greater cause of dis-
turbance than the barking of the mastiff chained
in the mill yard. They looked up in clear starlight
at the frowning battlements of the castle, and
daybreak found them in a hamlet on the Braes of
Doone. When beyond the Fords of Frew and the
Highland line, Foster could in some degree relax
his precautions, though he still journeyed in the
night. The Highland lairds held different opinions,
and were not altogether to be trusted. The name
of Argyll was great in those parts; and it was only
when he had skirted the country of the Campbells
and passed the Blackmount that he could afford to
laugh at the law.

But the condition of the prisoner caused him
no little anxiety. Strong man as he was, and
indifferent to the sufferings of other people, he
marvelled how she could bear up against the
inevitable hardships, against the fits of depression
in which strength seemed at the lowest ebb, and
the fitful gusts of passion which shook her to the
soul. He trembled, with reason, for the result.
Lovat might count even murder a good piece of
service, but it was a service which would be surely

repaid by making the accomplice the scapegoat. Life for life had been the charge when the lady was given over to his custody. And he had accepted the charge with his eyes open, knowing well that his worshipful lordship counted on disease or sudden death, on the hundred chances of Highland travel at that inclement season. In the rude quarters in the glens it was often difficult to obtain the bare necessaries. The coarse and scanty fare sufficed for the hardy Highlanders, but it revolted the delicately nurtured woman, consumed with burning fever, and maddened with mental anguish. How to deliver his failing charge in safety was the question, and Foster was not to be envied as he groaned and shrank under the weight of his responsibilities.

The troubles thickened as the party moved northwards. It had set in for steady rain; the swollen rivers were coming down in speat, and in the rough ferryboats, managed by careless Celts or clumsy Lowlanders, there were but patched and rotten planks between the passengers and sudden death. When the rope was loosed, and the raft-like cobble, with the terrified ponies, committed to the stream, there was suspense till it fetched the farther bank, perhaps some hundred yards lower down. As for the lady, Foster began at last to believe that she was set upon spiting him by a suicide. For his own sake and hers he redoubled his watchfulness; sometimes he deemed it needful to wrap her as before from head to foot in the swathings of a plaid, for the eloquence of her pleading eyes had seemed to rouse the ferrymen to something like a show of interference. Both he and she were on the alert, though with very different feelings. So long as they were among the people of Lowland speech, the alarm might be given and he might be compromised; whereas she knew that if she once passed the Highland line without leaving some clue, her fate was sealed and hope might be abandoned.

It rained, and still it rained, as they followed the course of the flooded Lyon, and passing beneath the limes of Meggernic, plodded upwards through the passes of the Blackmount. Foster, in his haste and anxiety, made no halt at Meggernic, though the laird was notoriously one of the disaffected. He would only breathe freely when he had plunged into the solitudes of Glencoe, where the law-writs had seldom run since the massacre, and where the southern speech was left far behind.

It rained, and still it rained, as they approached the gloomy portal giving access to the grim Valley of Weeping, where winter lasts for nine months in the year, and the summer passes like a gleam of sunshine between showers. Nothing was to be seen of the appalling sublimity of the mountains, though indeed none of the travellers would have regarded it from the picturesque point of view. The rain came down more and more heavily; each man as he dashed the drops from his eye-lashes could barely distinguish the croup of the pony in front. But from behind the curtain of falling water there came strange and mysterious sounds. There were the roar of the cataracts and the rush of the tumbling torrents, the scream of the eagle and the croak of the raven, and now and again the wild bellowing of a startled drove of black cattle, that had clambered down to seek shelter in the depths of the abyss.

For an abyss it was, and at the best of times the only path lay along the brink, and sometimes almost in the bed of the Coe. Now the river was rising fast, and even the Highlanders who followed Foster began to show signs of uneasiness or actual fear. They were superstitious, and rude as they were, they did not fancy the mission with which they were charged. They had been struck by the captive's strange personality and glowing eyes; and there was something that was uncanny about her; nor had the anxiety of their leader escaped them. One of them caught at the shoulder of a comrade.

"Did you hear that, Duncan? It sounds like the cry of the kelpie. There will be a drooned corpse or more before the morning, if we do not come the sooner to some sheltered bield. And the ill-favoured corbies are gathering in for the feast."

"Huts, man, with your kelpies and corbies," answered Duncan valiantly, but, nevertheless, he shuddered, and Foster, though less subject to superstitious tremors, began to feel seriously uneasy. He would have given much for a local guide, but they had seen neither herdsman nor hunter since they had entered the greyness of the glen. Sending one of his people in advance, he

rode himself behind his charge. He would have
kept a hand on her bridle, but that was impossible,
for no two animals could pass abreast. The dizzy
track, such as it was, was broken here and there
by the earth-slips, and from the right, above the
rushing of the rain, there came the roar of the
swollen Coe. Progress would have been impossible, except for the sure-footed shelties, who
scrambled like cats over boulders and breaches,
and always seemed to have a leg to spare. But
then there came a sound out of the darkness, as
if someone had tilted a cartload of gravel. A
guttural Gaelic oath, followed by a hoarse cry
of horror, and the lady in front of him
vanished, silent and spectre-like. Game to the
last, as it flashed upon him, she had gone and
made no sign.

But he remembered the warning, "Your life
for hers," and in a moment he was on his feet
between the hill and the pony. The slight shock
upset the poor animal's equilibrium, and, following
its fellow, it plunged down into the abyss. Foster
was not long behind, though he went more heed-
fully. Trusting himself to his strong hands, and

seeking hasty foothold, he safely effected a descent he might havo hesitated over on a clear day, and in cold blood. The swirling water was washing round his legs as he paused on a slippery ledge. He could dimly see some dark object in the back-swirl of the pool, and he plunged to the sound of a choking sob. He rose with a grip on the lady's garments. With the first clutch at him, presence of mind came back, and she trusted horself pas-sively to his arm. Surely the conspirators she terrorized had done prudently in sending such a woman into exile. Encumbered with his burden and his soaking clothes, Foster, though a powerful swimmer, had a hard fight for their lives. Nothing could have saved them but a back-flow in the pool. With help from above, by the aid of knotted plaids and saddle-girths, they were placed in safety on the farther side of the landslip. As for the unlucky advance-guard and the ponies, never were they seen or heard of again. But Foster gave small heed to their fate: his sole thought was to extricate the sur-vivors from their perilous dilemma. There was no discharging the firearms, for the flints were drenched, but the party were bidden to shout simultaneously.

"Curse these MacDonalds, the children of the mist and the devil, they cannot all have gone to earth with the brocks and the foxes; surely some of the men must be stirring if we could only get them to hear."

And speedily a loud halloo gave assurance of rescue. Ten minutes more, and they were guided to a cluster of hovels, where they received hearty and hospitable welcome. In the best of the humble shealings a shock-headed savage, nevertheless wearing the bonnet with the hawk's feather to indicate his gentility, was doing the honours with much natural courtesy. He scrupulously averted his eyes from the lady, whose presence mystified him, for curiosity might have been deemed a breach of good manners. But the prematurely shrivelled old woman who called him husband, and a couple of buxom though high-featured daughters were soon gathering the peats into a cheerful blaze; the collops of venison were frizzling in the frying-pan, and fresh oaten cakes were being baked on the girdle. The men withdrew to another of the huts while the lady changed her dripping garments. She supped charily, but did not refuse the quaich

of usquebagh ; and when she lay down on a bed
of heather, beneath the plaids of the family, over-
taxed nature asserted its rights, and she sunk into
deep and dreamless sleep.

When Foster came in the morning to ask after
her health, he was taken aback by his reception.
Hitherto there had been open hostility between
captive and guardian : now she frankly extended
her hand. Early as the visit was she had had time
to think out the situation. He took the proffered
hand hesitatingly and mistrustfully. Had he been
anything of a scholar, as Lovat was, he might
have exclaimed, " Timeo Danaos." .

" I owe you my life : I should have been food for
the fishes or the ravens," she said simply, by way
of explanation.

" Aye, truly, my lady, and that I should have
said yesterday, was the last good office for which
you would have thanked me. God knows the
sorrow and the sore vexation it's been to me, to
strive to keep you alive in spite of yourself."

" God knows it, and I know it ; but if you will
but do me another kindness, I'm willing to make
a bargain. I promise you that I'll live, and you

may dismiss all fear about it, if you will only agree to forward a message for me. And I never go back from my word," she added, with cold deliberation, "as some who bear themselves proudly, like honourable folk, may yet have good reason to know."

"By God, I believe it madam, I would trust you, and I can guess your meaning; but though I would gladly whistle with an easy mind on the march, and sleep sound after the seventh tumbler, the message would be more than my life is worth."

"Listen to me, man. I mean no harm to Lovat —not now at least, and it is only to him that your allegiance is due; you owe none, as I fancy, to my Lord of Grange."

"Far from it: rather the other way. My Lord of Grange, like his brother, will play cat in the pan with any in Scotland. I owe him one ill-turn already, or I am the more mistaken."

"Well, then," said the lady, speaking eagerly, "you may safely help me with no hurt to yourself. Hark ye, I know him well, and villain as he may be, he is cursed with a conscience. At this moment he is trembling at shadows in broad day, and starting up in the night from troubled slumbers. I would merely lay blisters upon smarting sores by reminding him again that he will have to reckon with the day of retribution."

"All very well, madam," said Foster, who had never fancied his mission, and began to feel some sympathy with the vengeful lady. "All very well, but bethink you, the message may be your death warrant."

"I tell you again, you do not know him. For the peace of mind he values and will never know again, he will never consent to have me murdered. I doubt if, on second thoughts, he would not be grateful for your saving me yesterday; otherwise my Lord Justice might have to condemn himself for being art and part in a deadly crime. And for your safety, the more mysteriously the message reaches him, the better. If he cannot trace the hand of man, he will be more ready to see the finger of God."

"It's a devil's prank you would play him, that's sure; and so a bargain be it. If I can find a trusty messenger, as I think I can, the thing is as good as done. The ploy may cost me a cast of

K

a rope, or a stab of a skene-dhu, or maybe a moon-light plunge in the black pool of the Beauly. But, yet, it's a grand jest to play off upon Grange, and if his own fingers be not scalded in the boiling broth, I know no one who would like it better than my lord of Lovat."

CHAPTER X.

INDEED, Lord Grange, in a different way, had already suffered scarcely less than his victim. Her spirit of vengeance might have been soothed, if not satiated, had she known all which she only suspected. The respected lay leader of the Ultra-Presbyterians lost flesh and colour. The ruddiness that came of hard drinking was sicklied by the pale cast of thought. The greetings in the market-place were frequent still, although some of his former friends showed him cold countenances; but ill-timed condolences stung him like serpents.

"Eh! my good lord, but I'm wae to see you looking but poorly; the loss of her ladyship is a sad calamity."

He suspected even his sycophants and parasites of concealing a sneer or hinting a doubt. Officious cronies were ever ready to acquaint him of the many malevolent whispers that were abroad.

K 2

When the wine had gone round the board for an hour or two, he began to fear he might be betrayed into indiscretions, yet he craved for drink to bring temporary oblivion. Her ladyship knew him well. He would start at shadows in the broad daylight, and when he reluctantly sought his couch, he knew he would awaken from dreams of horror in the small hours. One night he had slept well and awakened late. He passed into the breakfast parlour in good spirits, and scarcely glanced at a thumbed and weather-stained letter. But when he opened it negligently afterwards, he winced as if a wasp had stung him. Well did he know the familiar writing, which brought back a rush of mingling memories. In half-an-hour he had come to the resolution he had been hesitating over. "This cannot endure," he said to himself, "or I shall go raving mad. I must seek advice and make a clean breast of it somewhere. Better be made a spectacle now to men and angels, than burn eternally."

He swallowed a great bumper of brandy and walked forth with cocked hat and gold-headed cane, to find the minister and occasional boon companion whose ministrations he attended. But the many passengers who saluted him in the streets remarked the strange glitter of his eyes and the far-away look with which he acknowledged their greetings. For, as he walked, the wary old lawyer bethought himself; and in his confession he named no name, and made many reservations. The clean breast was out of the question with him, and he was incapable of committing himself when it came to the point.

The worthy minister lost patience at last, and forgot his reverence for the rank and station of his penitent.

"No physician can pronounce, my good lord, unless the patient submits himself to a searching examination. You say that the secret is not your own, and that it concerns grave matters of high policy. It may be so, but then you need not have come to me. I can only guess, and it may be I guess aright. I will never believe that you hold with the damnable Jesuitical doctrine, that the end justifies the means. But this I say, in the name of our Master, that if you have done grievous wrong to any living soul, reparation must come before repentance, and that the Achan who has hidden away an accursed thing, must make confession and dree his penance before he gets back his peace."

So Grange got less than little consolation, and left his adviser in an excessively carnal state of mind. "Damn the minister with his Achans, and his Babylonish garments, when a word of good comfort might have helped a friend. The more fool I to take him fasting before the meridian, instead of seeking his counsel after supper. Reparation before repentance!—aye, but that's for ever sticking in my thrapple."

He had acquired a convenient habit of swearing piously at large, while his features expressed gravity and benignity, and no one could have suspected the storm raging within, as the reverend seigneur paced back to his lodgings. This passive endurance with the sword ever hanging over his head was intolerable. The sole remedy was action in some shape—action which might possibly lead to reparation.

"By G—" he exclaimed, aloud, "I'll go North and have another talk with Simon. His wit may find a way out of the wood, and, anyhow, I will be the better for the change and the travel."

      *   *   *   *   *

Even in the summer time a ride from Edinburgh
to Inverness was no light undertaking for an
elderly gentleman. But use is everything : horseback with the servant and sumpter beast behind,
was the only means of travel—the Judges of Assize
went circuit in the saddle—and Lord Grange set forth
manfully on his progress. His spirits rose rapidly,
for they were lightened by fair accommodation and
the best of good company. Most nights he " lay " in
the house of some laird or nobleman of " honest "
principles, who made much of the illustrious guest
who had drawn up the memorandum from the
Highland chiefs submitted by Mar to King George
before the rising. The Whigs were scarcely less cor-
dial in their welcome, for Grange came recommended
by his zeal for Presbyterianism. And when he un-
buckled his mails in some change house, he brought
a well-stored provision basket, and found company
and sport for his wit in the parish minister or school
teacher. Already he was another man when his
eyes wandered over the fertile Aird, stretching along
the broad estuary of the Beauly, and he saw the
white-washed turrets and bartizans of Castle Downie,
looking down on the older fortalice of Lovat.

His arrival had been duly announced and his friend was ready to receive him with all honour. MacShimei in his swelling tartans, with his tail behind him, and encompassed by semi-barbaric courtiers, was a very different man from the Lovat of the lodgings in the Lawnmarket and Fortune's tavern. He welcomed his old friend and fellow-conspirator with the ceremonious dignity of a Louis Quatorze. It was only when he ushered him under the gloomy gateway that he slapped his shoulder and whispered a jest in his ear. The stronghold of the Highland kinglet was characteristic of the man and the times. Unlike the Tudor or Queen Anne architecture of peaceful England, it was built to withstand storm or siege. The massive walls of solid masonry, some fourteen feet thick, were hollowed out here and there for a tiny chamber, and in each of the several stories was a single apartment of considerable size. The chieftain's truckle bed stood in a corner of his dining-room. The narrow windows had been arranged for defence rather than convenience, and when the sun was the brightest the light filtered in through narrow passages like drain-pipes or rabbit burrows. Below ground,

in the rock on which the tower was built, the
accommodation was ample, if even less commodious.
There were dungeons absolutely dark, or only illuminated and ventilated by slits : and the lowest were
oubliettes, to which the only access was by raising a
flagstone let into the roof.   Lovat, who was sheriff
of the county as well as chief of his clan, exercised
despotic authority with certain constitutional limi-
tations.   An unpopular ukase might have led to his
summary deposition.   But so long as he flattered
his courtiers and kept the commons generally in
good humour, he might work his will on individuals
and only strengthen his authority.   As a De Gram-
mont or De Tremorille, who incurred the displeasure
of the Grand Monarque, might be sent straight
from Versailles to the Bastille on a *lettre de cûchet*,
so if any one of his clansmen crossed Lovat's will,
he might be dropped from the dinner table into
a dungeon to rot, unless he sought release by
plenary submission.   In the boisterous carouse
men still kept a guard on their lips, when the
smiling chieftain was sitting within earshot.

But Grange came there as an honoured guest,
and gave no thought to the sighing of the prisoners

in the basement. To do Lovat justice, nothing could exceed his open-handed hospitality—indeed, it was an essential part of his sagacious policy. The stalkers were out on the hills, the fishermen and fowlers were abroad on the streams and lochs; the lord's own wealth consisted in great measure in the herds of black cattle and the flocks of sheep, and the tenants paid the best part of their rents in kind—in meat and meal, dairy produce, and poultry. No need to describe the style of housekeeping, though, indeed, " housekeeping " is a misnomer, for most of the feasting and drinking went on out of doors. If Scott did not paint Waverley's reception at Glennaquoich from the customs of Castle Downie, all that can be said is that we are strangely mistaken.

Now and again, early in the first evening, Grange approached the subject which had brought him to the North. But his host warned him off with good-humoured *bonhomie*. " It's ill talking, you know, between a full man and a fasting, and be your business what it may, it will surely keep till to-morrow."

Nor was Grange altogether unwilling to be put off. His health and spirits had improved with the journey. He almost marvelled that he had ever been moved to undertake it, and he was ready enough to make the best of the passing hour.

Lovat seemed all smiles and joviality, but really he was in a diabolical temper. The followers, who knew his moods, trembled when he turned his smiling eyes on them. He flattered himself on his system of *espionnage*, on his having ears and eyes all over Scotland, but for once his trusted agents had failed him. He had had but a short twenty-four hours' notice of Grange's arrival, which he had affected to welcome as a joyful surprise. He knew well what his lordship had come about ; he made a shrewd guess at the motives ; and as the captive happened to be in keeping in the Island of Aigas, within no long ride of the Castle, he had made haste to get on the safe side and hustle her out of the country. Grange woke late the next morning, with aching head and muddled brains, for he had honoured many a toast and been plied with potent liquor. Lovat had been up two hours before him, had already sentenced some culprits brought up for justice, had received the assurance that Lady Grange would that morning be on her way towards the West, and had arranged his ideas for the impending interview which he was now as determined to provoke as he had previously been resolved to defer. It was Grange who would now have hung back, for, with his wits gone a wool-gathering, he knew that his friend Simon could befool him to will. Nor was he mistaken. Lovat, with a great show of hearty interest, speedily turned him inside out. Even Grange's reticences, for the habit of caution was instinctive, were so many revelations. Lovat heard all about the seeking absolution from the Church, with the narrow miss of making full confession— and if wishes would have killed, his friend was doomed and dead. But what with sophistry, mockery, and cogent, practical arguments, Grange was brought to a reasonable frame of mind. His scruples were absurd, though they did him honour ; but the path of duty and piety was plain.

"That tender heart of yours is your worst enemy, my good lord. You tempered justice with mercy when a life was fairly forfeited, but further weakness would be criminal. I am bound to say, besides, it would be clear treachery, and nothing less, to all

who are banded with you in the common cause, and
who are venturing so much for your life and credit.
I could show you letters from Dunvegan and
Sleat. Do you think that men like MacLeod and
MacDonald will be content to have their necks
knotted up in your lady's apron strings? You
have done well and wisely as yet, if you have been
somewhat weak—forgive my frankness, but we are
old and tried friends, and now the matter is out of
our hands, and we may wash them of all responsibility. The lady went West weeks ago, to Mac-
Leod's country. You will not doubt his word, and
he has passed it for her safety and all reasonable
observance ; but if I know aught of that son-in-law
of mine, he is not the chiel to let her go when her
flight would put his craig in jeopardy. The book
is closed and your mind may be easy, so now let
us to dinner."

So far, so well. Supper followed dinner in due
course ; the friends kept it up later than before ;
Grange was carried to bed, decidedly more drunk,
but awoke less dazed and mentally more comfortable. His servant called his attention to a note
on the table, secured to the planks by a rusty clasp-

knife, in the fashion of the agents of the fatal Vehmgericht. It was pretty nearly a duplicate of the missive which had worked trouble up to fever heat in his Edinburgh lodging. It was written in my lady's well-known hand; moreover, it was dated but two days before from Eilean Aigas. Then Lovat had lied to him on one point; probably he had deceived him on others. He sought his host in high dudgeon, tempered by wholesome apprehension. It was awkward for even a Lord of Justiciary to beard in his own hall a man who had shown himself capable of any audacity. Grange's voice was tremulous, for he felt far from assured that he might not be summarily consigned to one of the dungeons, or—what was as likely—sent to keep company with his wife in the Western Isles. He was soon relieved on that score. Lovat, with inimitable self-possession, treated the matter of the missive as a jest, though a very bad one. "One of the long-eared loons, whom we were forced to let partly into our secrets, must have been hearkening behind the door and dared to play the prank when the malt had got abune the meal. I will seek him out and take order with him, and on that you may depend." Accordingly he left the chamber with a look of patriarchal austerity.

Then the storm broke. The dependents who had been unfortunate enough to see the chieftain in a rage, had seen a countenance of diabolical malignity. His wrath was the more terrible that the cold compression of the lips contrasted with the swollen veins of the forehead. He controlled himself, because he knew that his despotic power could gratify any refinements of vengeance. This was a family matter, to be settled quietly without taking his guest into his confidence. All his household whom he could suspect were passed under review, and underwent the searching ordeal of furious looks and incisive questioning. In some cases he affected to assume the guilt, but he had to confess that he was baffled. Treachery there must be among those he trusted, and such a thing had never happened before. And if *his* astuteness were fairly at fault, on whom could he rely for the future? He thought of a message of death to overtake the lady, but if that were done, Grange, in a paroxysm of suspicion and remorse, was like enough to turn King's evidence. Then the murder would be a mistake. He even thought of drugging the nightcap of his guest, but that would bring up a fresh crop of suspicions in unwelcome quarters; —was not Culloden keeping house, almost within gunshot?—and, moreover, he had Highland qualms as to the abuse of hospitality. Finally, he calmed himself somewhat in the meantime, by ordering half-a-dozen of the morning's culprits to be hung up by the heels to some dule trees within sight of the Castle windows.

CHAPTER XI.

PERILS AT SEA.

LADY GRANGE left Strathfarrar in a calmer frame of mind that she would otherwise have done, inasmuch as she had found means of shooting Parthian arrows which, as she fondly hoped, would make rankling wounds. Having flung away regard for a life which had become worthless, except in so far as it might serve her vengeance, she began to take a certain pleasure in playing at dice with death. Repeatedly she would have sought refuge in suicide, had she not lived on for her vengeance, and remembered her pledge to Foster. But, indeed, she felt that now she was playing on velvet, for she had the conviction that she must live to be avenged. Moreover, she was encouraged by having induced Foster to take a hand in her game. As she had won upon him, she might work upon others. As for Foster, he was grateful for her having saved him much trouble by keeping her

L

faith. He found relief from his wearisome duty in the company of a woman who could shorten the hours when she condescended to entertain him; nor, among the unkempt Highland lasses and shrivelled hags, was he insensible to her fading charms. For mountain air and a simple diet had done much to counteract hardships and mental misery. And having once betrayed his master with impunity—for the mistrustful Lovat still had absolute confidence in him—he had ventured to risk the second stroke. Done partly in a pure spirit of devilry, it had gratified his grudge against Grange beyond hope, and should have gone, besides, some considerable way towards the balancing of any accounts with Lovat.

Now he and the lady were to part, and at last he answered her frequent questions as to her destination, with deeper feeling and more delicacy than she would once have believed him capable of.

"My orders, and they must be obeyed—there is no help for that—are to see your ladyship shipped for the Western Islands."

Her ladyship heard him in the stolid despair which had become habitual. She rode forward, bowed over her saddle, lost in her own gloomy reflections, and saying no word, good or bad. "She's sore changed," thought Foster, "since the day we brought her away from West Lothian. Then she would have fought and skirled like a wild cat, but now——" The night was closing in upon them as the wearied ponies picked their steps down the precipitous path which led to Loch Hourn. The darkness had set in when they reached the bottom, and was but faintly illuminated by one or two flickering lights near at hand, and by another farther away, which seemed to be reflected in a shimmering mirror.

"Aye, that'll be the bark," said Foster, "and we will raise a flame by way of sign to them, for your ladyship will do better to sleep on board."

There was no answer. She suffered Foster to lift her from her pony, and she sat down upon the beach in sullen silence, till the stillness was broken by the plash of oars. The prow of a boat grounded on the gravel, and a figure stumbled on to the shore. Foster challenged: "Who goes there? Stand and answer."

"And who would it be, but Donald MacLeod that

you're seeking," was the answer, in stammering and guttural accents.

" And Donald MacLeod would have done better to keep sober, when he was expecting a lady of consideration, recommended by Lovat to his chief."

" So Donald would have done, had it pleased you to keep tryste. But we've missed the wind that would have wafted us to Hesker, and it would be news if you'd tell me what better was to be done but to birle the liquor about and empty the quaichs."

For Donald, who had made sundry voyages to Holland and France, where he had become as familiar with Schiedam and Cognac as with the Glen Tallisker, had made fair progress with the English.

Foster looked down on the bowed form of the lady, and checked the hasty answer which rose to his lips. For her sake he would not irritate the rough-spoken sailor who was to be her temporary keeper. He touched her shoulder and stooped to whisper—

" You must be gone, my lady, since better may not be. If my wishes can do any good, may

happier luck attend you. My counsel is to say little
the night, and speak soft. My belief is that this
MacLeod is a man you may lippen to, and when he's
had his sleep and come to his senses, you will not
find him lacking in civility. Moreover, he has his
commands from those he is bound to obey."

Seizing her under the arms he set her on her
feet, and, with a "Fare-ye-well," he pushed her
gently towards the boat and prepared to hand her
into it. Then she turned and clasped his hand.

"I shall live, maybe, to do you a service yet,
and anyhow I have a last request to make to you.
You have helped me twice, and may help me
again."

"Ask, anyway, madam, and if it be in my
power——"

"Twice have you pricked my lord with a poisoned
dagger; prick him ever again when you have the
opportunity, and should the occasion come, drive
the dagger to his heart."

"I'm but a plain man, my lady, and it may be
you are speaking parables, but as to stabbing a
Lord of Justiciary to the heart, it's clean and clear
out of the question. But if you mean that I am to

keep him secretly in mind of you, it's a ploy that will please me well, if your ladyship cares to run the hazard."

" You swear ? "

" I swear ; and now I must bid you a last good-night, for I see that the skipper is losing patience, and there may be trouble yet if he tynes temper as well."

In the first faint streaks of the dawn, the *Ina* was working out of Loch Hourn, assisted by the light landward breeze.   Had the skipper, a shrewd old sea-dog, been in full possession of his faculties, it may be questioned whether he would have sailed. The *Ina* was an old, half-decked sloop, with patched timbers and rotten cordage.   Her master knew exactly how far she might be trusted, nor was he one who in ordinary circumstances cared to run extraordinary risks.   Lady Grange had scarcely tried to sleep in the coffin-like bunk in the filthy cabin.   Yet towards late morning she had sunk into a troubled doze, from which she was roused by the uneasy motion.   The *Ina* had cleared the mouth of the loch, and was pitching rather than standing out to sea.   The light morning breeze was already dying down, and the broad-bottomed bark could barely hold its own against the heavy swell rolling in from the Atlantic. Quiet as it had been on the Scottish shore, there must have been stormy weather away to the westward. When the skipper was called by the three-handed crew, and came stumbling up from his couch at the bottom of the companion-ladder, after rubbing his eyes, the first thing he did was to call for a hair of the dog that had bitten him. Then he rubbed his eyes again and took a long look to seaward. His brows puckered anxiously as he addressed his second in command.

"What are ye making of it, Dugald, my man? Deil's in ye that ye did not call me sooner."

"Sure, and she's no liking it, whatever, Donald. I wuss now that ye had no bidden us put out from the loch."

Donald growled something in reply, and cast a wistful look at the mouth of the harbour. But already it had fallen dead calm, and there was no possibility of putting back. It was so calm that to the novice the only immediate danger would have seemed that of detention off a dangerous coast.

But to seaward these experienced mariners saw signs that were sufficiently disquieting. Beneath a long low bank of black cloud, a thin grey veil rising from the sea was blotting out the watery reflections of sunshine. The curtain rose, shutting out the clouds; it thickened, and came floating rapidly forward. In less space than would seem credible, the *Ina* was enveloped in the fog—a fog so dense, that from the little hatchway it was impossible to distinguish a figure at the bows. Through the watery greyness came uncanny sounds and mysterious moanings—the cries of the startled sea-fowl winging their flight to the land, and the broken murmur of the heavy surges as they seethed in the chasms of the rock-bound coast.

Alone, among a new set of strangers and persecutors, Lady Grange's overstrung nerves gave way. She had vowed she would have nothing to say to the drunken and brutal master, but now in natural weakness she caught hold of his homespun jacket and clung to him. He was more civil than might have been expected, and condescended to explain and reassure her. "There's no present peril, my lady, unless the wind should spring up and shift. I ken the currents fine, and they're aye carrying us away from the land. But it's a mischancy mist, there's no denying that, and Lord knows where we may be drifting to should it last."

As the day went on, the mist thinned and thickened alternately, but always they were in the drip of impenetrable vapour. The skipper would have lost his bearings in any case, but things were worsened by the fitful puffs of a wind which swayed them hither and thither, though far from strong enough to clear the air.

"Had we no better set a spark to a peat, and show it in the bit grate in the forecastle?" asked old Dugald.

"Heavens, man," was the answer, "you might as well show a light from your pipe, gin you could get the tobacco to burn."

So they stood on, or rather tossed about, trusting to Providence. There was but little traffic on those seas at that time, yet the skipper, moved, as it would appear, by some presentiment, kept anxious watch at the bow, peering out into the grimness.

"Aye, aye, I deemed as much," he muttered, as

he screened his eyes; and then he shouted like a Stentor—

" Shift your helm, man ; hard-a-port for the love of God. D—n you, Dugald, do you no hear me crying to you ? "

The helmsman acted promptly on the order, but the tub had scant steerage way, and refused to answer. All passed in a few seconds. Donald dancing on the poop in Celtic excitement, calmed down into Celtic fatalism, as the bows and fore-rigging of a far bigger ship than his own took shape and form as they bore slowly down on him.

Aboard the stranger all hands were alive and alarmed, but it was too late to avert the collision. The stranger ground slowly past with slow impact and far superior weight; the sloop's little stick of a bowsprit gave with a crash, and there was rasping and rending of timber. The stern of the stranger faded out of sight, and the skipper breathed a sigh of relief.

" It might have been waur, anyway, for we're always afloat and little mischief done." And when there came a hail, demanding if he wanted help, he merely answered by shaking his fist and swearing at large. He shouted loudly enough five minutes afterwards, but again it was too late. The *Ina* was settling down slightly at her head, and her skipper was up to his ankles in water. But though Donald had his weaknesses, he was of proved coolness and courage. One of the rotten planks had started, but all hands were speedily at work, stopping the leak with blankets and anything else.

"Ye'll be for putting back, if only the mist would lift," said Dugald, rather as matter of certainty than as a query. Now that was just what Donald intended to do, when the ill-timed suggestion set up his bristles.

"You will be looking to your own business, Dugald MacLeod," he said with much dignity, "and leave me to attend to mine. Is it to Hourn that we are sailing, do you think, or is it to Hesker?"

Dugald knew his man, and said no more. He contented himself with grumbling to his fellows, "If it should come on to blow this night, and there's a sough of storm in the wet, it is to the bottom, maybe, and not to Hesker that we will be going." So Donald was hardened in his reckless purpose by unwonted murmurs of mutiny on board.

Sure enough it did come on to blow. The broad stern of the labouring old craft caught the fierce gusts that drove her forward, dipping her bows in the seas that broke over her in clouds of spray and foam. The timbers groaned below: there was crashing and splintering of the rotten bulwarks. The primitive pumps were manned; the men stripped to their shirts and toiled for dear life; but still the water gushed clearer and clearer from the scuppers, and the *Ina* threatened to be water-logged. The whisky, served out freely, ceased to have any effect, and the hands, knocking off from their fruitless labours, were resigning themselves with Celtic fatalism. If they ceased pumping, their fate was sealed.

The Lady Grange had never a fairer chance of getting rid of her troubles without a shadow of guilt. The kindly surges of the Atlantic would have released her from the faith she had solemnly plighted to Foster. Yet now that death was staring her in the face, she was seized with an overwhelming longing for life. It was not that she dreaded the hereafter and judgment; still less that she desired to live for revenge. At the moment she gave no

thought to any of those things. She simply
shrank from the immediate horror of being engulfed
in that dismal greyness, and shrouded in that
raging ocean. But the fear acted like a tonic on
her nerves, and roused her high spirit to passionate
exertion. She struggled up the little scuttle and
stood on the slippery deck among the despairing
seamen, holding fast to a shroud. There was
something like a temporary lull, and her voice
sounded shrilly in the comparative stillness.

"Fools and cowards that you are, you have made
up your minds for the bottom, but hearken to me.
You have read the Scriptures, all of you, and you
mind how Paul said to the soldiers when he was
being shipwrecked, ' Unless these abide in the ship,
you cannot be saved.' I tell you what you ken
well yourselves, unless you stick to the pumping
you cannot be saved. If you will use the means
our safety is certain. Our safety, I say, for your
lives are bound up with mine, and I speak the
words of truth and certainty. It has been revealed
to me that I am not doomed to die to-night, and so
I bid you all be of good courage."

The superstitious Highlanders who had thought

of their passenger as a she-Jonah, although they understood little of her language, changed their minds immediately, as they caught courage from her face, illuminated by the faint light of the lantern attached to the mainstay. They raised a feeble cheer, but again betook themselves to the pumps. Then, all at once, as it were by enchantment, the sunshine broke through the mist. The dense sea-fog thinned and lifted. They saw a sign from heaven, and turning to, they worked with a will. With the fall of the water in the hold, they found the worst of the leaks, and plugged it with their plaids and the lady's feather bed. The low-lying shores of Hesker were seen ahead; sweeps were put out; the *Ina* was piloted into the half land-locked harbour, and run aground on the shelving beach, whence she might be floated off at a springtide. The captain was full of gratitude, for the lady had saved life and ship and credit, and the sailors were content to be thankful for their lives.

Assigned to the man in charge who represented MacLeod, as a forlorn captive who was a stumbling-block in the way of the chief, Lady Grange stepped ashore in an odour of sanctity. Mysterious whispers of the rough mariners told how she was in closest communion with heaven, and gifted with something far above the ordinary second-sight. So the ignorant islanders were ready to worship her, and even the better educated headman, and the Gaelic-speaking schoolmaster were inclined to regard her with reverence chastened with fear.

CHAPTER XII.

HESKER.

THE time dragged on in the desolate seclusion of Hesker. It was confinement almost on the silent system in a dreary prison, with walls of water and perpetual mists. The few inhabitants spoke nothing but the Gaelic, and the captive could only communicate by signs. The sole exceptions were the tacksman and his wife, who had a smattering of the English, but they were mistrustful and inclined to be unfriendly. They were well-meaning but narrow-minded folk, and the lady had been given into their custody with a cloud on her character and fame. With Scottish caution they did not seek to dispel the mystery, for they had had a significant hint against asking questions. She was left to the brooding thoughts which must have made a weaker woman an idiot or lunatic, but otherwise her lot was not intolerable. Her abode was a stone-built cottage with glazed

windows, and if the fare was homely it was
plentiful enough. A chest of the clothes she had
left behind in West Lothian had been duly
forwarded, and by chance, or for kindness, some
books had been thrown in. There were a Shakspeare, and the "Essay on Criticism" of Mr.
Pope; some remains of a stray volume of "The
Spectator," and what she valued next to a Bible,
the "Pilgrim's Progress." Probably these books
saved her reason; but it was the Bible that the
woman who was sustained by an inextinguishable
hope of revenge chose as the habitual companion
of her solitary rambles. She shrunk from the
New Testament, with its exhortations to love,
charity and repentance, though there were times
when she had to resist irrepressible yearnings.
She had an idea that it was there she might seek
for peace, but that peace was incompatible with her
fixed purpose. She had yet years to live as she
was assured, and peace might follow penitence on
the fruition of her righteous vengeance. And
surely the Old Testament was equally inspired.
What she loved were the ruthless deeds of Hebrew
champions and heroines; the slaughter of Sisera,

M

the assassinations of Eglon and Holofernes, and
above all, the grand catastrophe when the blinded
Samson involved himself and his task-masters
in a common fate.   What pleased her in the
Psalms were the passionate outbreaks, where the
sweet singer of the churches invokes all manner
of calamities on the heads of his enemies.   Saints,
prophets, and law-givers had left her examples
which fully justified her treading in their steps.

Pervert the spirit of the Scriptures as she might,
her frequent study of the well-known volume
with its brazen clasps added immensely to her
reputation for sanctity.   From year's end to year's
end the islanders seldom saw a priest, and they
would have sought her intercession, had they been
able to address her.   She had used to advantage
some simple drugs she had received, and she got
general credit for working miracles.   The very
frivolities with which she sought to while away
the weary hours imposed on the reverence of
the unsophisticated folk.   Sometimes she would
indulge in the melancholy pleasure of tricking
herself out in the spangled brocades she had worn
at festivities at Preston and in Edinburgh.   Then

with her mature charms renovated by abstinence and sea air, with her wealth of silver-streaked hair arranged in a towering coronet, she broke on the dazzled senses like a celestial vision. Never could the untutored fancies of the Hesker barbarians have decked the Virgin herself in such unconceivable splendour.

The upshot of all which was that the tacksman grew intolerably uneasy. Leaving strict charge with his wife to keep careful watch, he made a special expedition to Dunvegan to lay the case before his chief. The people held the lady for a saint, and were inclining to do her bidding at a word. If the word could have been spoken, she might have been gone ere now. But signs might take the place of spoken speech, and for his part he would no longer be answerable for anything. Even if he were awake in the night, as well as through the day, he could not always have an eye on all the berlins.*

"Am I not their chief, and have you not told them my will?" demanded MacLeod, imperiously.

But the chieftain was only *primus inter pares*

* The boats of the islanders.

M 2

with the dhunewassels who claimed kindred, and the sturdy tacksman held his own.

"Chief you are," and he bowed with a reverent flourish of his bonnet, "but it's God's truth that this woman has got a most extraordinary grip of them; and they think that heaven is nearer to Hesker than Dunvegan. I have said my say, MacLeod, and I cleanse my hands of all wight and blame. It's my pleasure and my bounden duty to do your bidding to the best of my ability, but I give you fair warning that in my poor mind the woman is fell likely to slip through our fingers."

Had she done so, MacLeod would perhaps have been content to run the risk. He disliked the invidious office of head gaoler, and personally he could be but indirectly implicated in any revelations. But he dreaded the wrath of his formidable father-in-law, for Lovat ruled his allies with a rod of iron. His nearest of kin could never trust him. The revelations of Lady Grange might leave MacLeod unharmed, but there might be matter enough in the *écritoires* of Castle Downie to beggar his estate if not to cost him his head. So despatches were forwarded to Edinburgh and

Inverness which threw Grange into aggravated paroxysms of anxiety, and gave Lovat food for serious reflection. Again the old plotter reflected ruefully that your only sure place of confinement is the grave, and he lamented the ugly caprices of Dame Fortune, giving the misguided woman a charmed life. It should have been so easy to put her out of the way with scarce the shadow of a suspicion. Now she was doubly guarded—by the scruples of Grange, and by the honour of MacLeod, which was not to be tampered with. Complacent he might have been, for love or fear, but nothing would induce him to be accomplice in a murder. And he knew Lovat too well to let the captive out of his keeping without taking due precautions for her safety, after consenting for years to act as her custodian.

"God d—n MacLeod, for a hot-headed, honourable fool! If he will care for her so tenderly, he shall keep her still." And the result of it was letters to Grange and to Dunvegan, in which he expressed his will, rather than recommended a course of procedure.

*   *   *   *   *

In the British Isles and their surroundings—
scarcely on the habitable globe—is there a more
out-of-the-way spot than the rock of St. Kilda? It
lies far apart from the great waterways of communication, and before the introduction of steam it
was seldom sighted by a passing ship. Now and
again a pirate or a privateer might see its perilous
cliffs to shun them, or a crippled vessel might be
driven out of its course; but the wrecks were only
few and far between, and were welcomed and long
remembered as godsends. The sole intercourse of
the aborigines with the outer Hebrides was once in
the year or so, when the master's factor came to
collect revenues that were paid from the feathers of
the sea-fowl. These gentle savages were content
with their lot; and they never fathomed the depths
of their poverty, for in their ignorance they had
no dreams of more blissful existence. Their barren
rock offered bare subsistence at the best of times,
and they patiently endured the times of starvation,
with the sickness that followed, when the yearly
ship failed to import the expected supplies. Disease
ran its course, save for the treatment by simples of
the herbalists, with traditional recipes, and the

wise women with their incantations. There was no
doctor, of course, and the minister was a catechist,
who, having failed to pass his trials for the Church,
had been gradually lowering himself to the level of
his parishioners. Death had slight terrors for
them, for they were face to face with it hourly in
their every-day occupations, whether fowling on
the precipitous cliffs or running out their fishing
lines from frail boats on the ocean, where a storm
might come as a surprise to boatmen who knew
nothing of the barometer. Lovat dared not dismiss
his victim to the grave, but he did the next best
thing for himself and friends in dooming her to
dismal reclusion on St. Kilda.

She should have been hardened to shocks and
habituated to surprises. Yet it was like tearing up
the roots from a relatively tranquil existence when
she was roused one morning at Hesker, with no
previous warning, to be hurried with her belongings
on board such a vessel as had carried her over from
Loch Hourn. A pang was added to the wrench of
the parting when her humble worshippers pressed
forward to kiss her hands, or knelt in groups on
the sands to invoke blessings on her head. Yet,

on second thoughts, the pain was not only alle-
viated, but changed to a sense of such pleasure as
when a sore is smarting with genial heat, on the
application of the healing ointment. It was a new
experience—in these latter years at least—to be
adored and loved and mourned. When the lamentations rose into howls, as the vessel widened its
distance from the shore, they sounded like music
in her ears as they consoled her with vague possi-
bilities.

And she needed consolation. She had no fear
for her life, had she given a thought to it. She
was still assured she must survive to fulfil her
destiny. Nevertheless she was full of pressing
anxieties. She was to change the prison to which
she had become half-reconciled, but how could she
change the desolate Hesker for the worse? If she
had illusions as to being taken back towards
civilization, they were speedily dispelled. The
little vessel spread her tarry canvas and headed
for the westward. Had it been bigger and better
found, she might have fancied she was being
banished to the Plantations; but in the circumstances such a fancy was out of the question.

Then, for the time, with the pitching and tumbling
on the seas, with the foul atmosphere of the close
little cabin, the sickness that prostrated her made
her indifferent to everything. The master of the
craft had waited upon her with rough kindness,
and ere now she had become well used to male
attendance. In the morning he came to her with
a pannikin of tea—then an unfamiliar luxury in
these parts—and bade her dress and come upon
the deck, for the sea had gone down and the
schooner was tacking landwards in the shelter of
a lee-shore.

"What land?" the lady demanded eagerly, but
the seaman only shook his shaggy head and beat a
hasty retreat.

When she came on deck, everything around her
was shrouded in the floating gossamer of thin grey
vapour. To the westward a faint golden radiance
was glistening through the veils; overhead and to
the south she caught imperfect glimpses of a
jagged peak or two towering above the haze.
Then as the glowing orb rose out of the ocean,
in the unclouded splendour of his fresh morning
brightness, the mists were dispersed and the

shadows fled away. She looked around on such a fairy scene of stern and imposing beauty as she had never seen or imagined. It had nothing in common with the sombre grandeur of Glencoe, or the lowering gloom that brooded over Loch Hourn. She saw such a fantastic palace of the Tritons and sea-nymphs as Staffa, but on a far more colossal scale. It was Nature's own Gothic architecture—stupendous and grimly imposing. In front and to right and left were the superb but shadowy outlines of frowning cliff and rugged promontory, of beetling headland and darksome recess. A craggy islet, separated from the main island by a narrow strait, showed like a rambling feudal fortress with its central keep and flanking towers, and an archway apparently giving access to the stronghold, through which the surges rushed tumultuously. Stacks or sharp-pointed needles rose in clusters, indicating the hidden perils of the broken water that guarded the embattled isle, where domes and columns, flashing through the rising mists, soared above the steep rock-wall into the gorgeous confusion of cloudland. It was impossible to distinguish between the actual and the apparent. And as the sun rose higher, and the cliffs caught the reflections of his beams, they were seen to be clothed in a rich variety of colour. The dead white of the sheer face of some precipice, or the shelves that were whitened with the droppings of the sea-birds, were relieved by patches of blazing crimson or resplendent orange.

And those seafowl! The scene was impressive enough in the appalling sense of desolate solitude, but it was very far from silent. The outlying sentinels, woke up from their night watch on the waves, or disturbed in their distant fishing expeditions, had given the alarm long before. The myriads of winged inhabitants were on the lookout, and when the schooner dropped anchor off a natural jetty, they unanimously roused themselves in fierce indignation to resent the intrusion on their loneliness. Ere the natives had awakened to the miracle of this most unexpected visit, the air was darkened with clouds of screaming sea-fowl, swarming like mosquitoes over an African swamp. Each species took its part in the far-resounding orchestra: the shrill treble of the puffins, the sharper tenor of the guillemots, blending with the

impassioned scolding of the gulls, and the deep bass
of the cormorants; while the solan geese chimed
in with their harsh croaking expostulations. Now
the chorus swelled into ear-piercing clamour; now,
as the feathered clouds receded, and the bass of
the cormorants prevailed, it sank into a sad wailing
dirge. The wild and mournful music did not tend
to raise the lady's depressed spirits, yet there
was some sensation of pleasure in any change;
and now that the mists had gone, and the island
was flooded in sunshine, she saw green pastures
in narrow cliff-enclosed glens, with sheep and cattle
that were peacefully homelike. The irrepressible
elasticity revived which had tided her already over
so many troubles. And again there was the lively
bustle of disembarking, nor was it without an
inspiriting dash of danger.'

The sea was comparatively still; nevertheless,
no inconsiderable ground-swell was rolling landward. The schooner had come as near the shore
as was compatible with safety. She saw pre-
parations to land by boat, and then a nearly
naked islander plunged into the surf. He swam,
strongfully and skilfully, like an eiderduck; now

breasting a wave and then letting another break
over him. When he scrambled up the side she
saw that he had a rope attached to him.

It was frayed and knotted here and there, for,
in fact, it was one of the two precious cables which
the natives used in their perilous fowling. It had
been secured to the prow of the boat on the beach;
the crew of the vessel hauled on it while the boatmen plied the oars, with yells chiming in with
the shrieks of the sea-fowl. The boat, with its
patched and rotten planks, was in worse condition
than the rope, and it seemed wonderful that it could
stand so strong a strain without having the bows
torn away bodily. Indeed, everything bespoke the
abject destitution of the islanders, down to the
tattered doublets of weather-bleached tartan, sometimes attached at the throat by a bone of the
fulmar. The chests of most of them were bare,
as were the heads and legs of all.

But Lady Grange had little time to make obser-
vations, ere she was handed down over the side;
her luggage followed, spite of the protests of the
St. Kildans, for, indeed, the leaky berlin was looking dangerously deep. They got to the shore safely,

nevertheless, with nothing worse than a thorough wetting. The lady was lifted out to leeward of the natural jetty, on shelving ledges slippery with sea wrack. As she picked her way among pools left by the tide, the captain, with unusual gentleness and gallantry, had always an arm at her service.

She was naturally impatient to see her new home. Her second impressions of the islanders were far from reassuring. The dress of the hard-featured women was wild as that of the men, and she remarked specially their sandals, which were fashioned out of necks of the solans, the feathery crest forming the heel. The island had seemed wonderfully fair from a distance, in its glory of natural domes and minarets; but as with many an imposing Oriental city, appearances were sadly deceptive. In the little hamlet which was the capital, with the score or two of houses dropped about at random, nothing could exceed the filth and squalor. There was an overpowering odour from the refuse of fish and fowl which rotted on the dungheaps among stagnant cesspools, for here were neither jackals or vultures to act as scavengers. Only the ventilation of the strong south-westerly winds could save the pestilential settlement from extermination. These were the prevalent winds in those parts, and the only uniform feature in the hovel architecture was that all the entrances looked to the north-east. Doors they could scarcely be called, for they were so low and narrow that even the stunted St. Kildans must bow themselves to enter. The captain remarked, with unfortunate suggestiveness, that if the houses were small she would find them all the cosier in the dark days and long nights of the winter.

"Doubtless," he said, "could MacLeod have sent news of your coming, more fitting preparation would have been made."

His intention was kindly, but it was hard to see how that could have been done. All the hovels were built like so many beehives, and resembled the huts of West African savages.

"However," the captain added cheerfully, after talking apart with some of the island notables, "one of the best of the houses can be got ready immediately. The man and his wife died of the sickness a week ago," he went on casually.

Lady Grange stooped low in involuntary abasement to enter her new tenement ; in fact—the onlookers deemed it an evil omen—she stumbled, and literally crawled in upon hands and knees. Within she could see nothing till her eyes accustomed themselves to the darkness. The only windows were small unglazed apertures in the massive walls of unhewn and uncemented stones. *En revanche*, the dwelling indicated its superiority to the others by the exceptional luxury of a smoke hole in the roof. There were two apartments. The outer, to senses of sight and smell, showed signs of having been recently occupied by cattle. In the inner was a rude fireplace and a box bed recessed in the slimy wall. Other furniture there was none ; but that, and the needful cooking utensils, the skipper assured her should be speedily supplied. There were pools of water on the earthen floor, and that luxurious chimney had its drawbacks, for the rain found its way in. Having acted as gentleman usher, the worthy seaman took his leave. "Time and tide, as you ken, my lady, will wait for no one,

and now that my business is despatched, I must get
sea room before it comes on to blow. It's a deevil
of a place, this St. Kilda, when the winds are
broken loose, and that your ladyship will find. But
God be with you, whatever befall."

With that blessing he was gone, and had the hovel
been less dim, she might have read unmistakable
compassion on the features of a man who was little
given to the gentler emotions. Again she felt the
wrench of parting from a friend, and nothing was
needed to aggravate her misery when she was left
to her reflections in the darkness. Here, in St.
Kilda, she was gagged and tongue-tied. There
was not a soul with whom she could hold
communion, or to whom she could make her com-
plaints intelligible, even if they could understand
her sufferings or alleviate them. If stricken down
by sickness, or if she fell a victim to despair, she
must die like a dumb beast, uttering inarticulate
moans. She had read of prisoners in the Bass or
the Bastille, and pitied them. They could at least
look forward to the visits of gaolers, who could hear
and be touched, and might possibly answer. She
pressed her hands on her throbbing temples, and

N

threw herself on the rude boards of the box bed,
where she sunk into a sort of stupor. It was the
troubled sleep compelled by a powerful anodyne
when the body is still racked by pain, and the
blood is simmering at fever heat.

She woke unrefreshed, to watch with dazed eyes
the sunbeams streaming through the hole overhead
and flickering in fantastic patterns on the puddles
in the floor. It was some little time before she
realized where she was, and then she fully awakened
to blank despair. Her cottage in Hesker was a
palace to this. Would her enemies never be weary
of persecuting her? Was it their purpose to drive
her mad before her plans could be accomplished?
Deliberate murder might be forbidden by her
husband's creed, but she thought she knew there
was nothing short of it to which he might not
stretch his conscience. Fool that she had been, not
to have anticipated him while they still kept up
the show of civility and when she had access to
the enemy's sleeping chamber, when his senses were
drugged by debauch. She had listened with disgust
to his stertorous breathing, though she shared his
vices as well as his bed; and the pressure of a pillow

might have done the work, without the shadow of a suspicion. It was maddening to think of those neglected opportunities, and as she tossed, she was half choked by her passion and her sobs. She sprung up, to rush into the open air, that she might draw breath more freely.

.

.

CHAPTER XIII.

THE LIFE IN ST. KILDA.

THE weary days and months dragged on, yet for a choice of sorrows, on the whole, perhaps, she had changed prisons for the better. In Hesker all had been tame, flat, and monotonous. In St. Kilda there was at least excitement and a strange novelty of surroundings. The involuntary excitement kept her alive, and the Atlantic breezes brought back the colour to her cheeks and elasticity to her step. It was true that the darkening days and the long winter nights were ineffably dismal, yet even these were killed, *tant bien que mal*, by the help of exercise, sleep, and books. She would walk and climb till fatigue brought weariness, and would drop asleep and forget her troubles for a time, as she pored over ill-printed pages by the dim light of a lamp fed with the rank fulmar oil. Happily those lustrous eyes of hers were good as ever. A great gulf divided her from the islanders, with whom she had few feelings in common; but nevertheless she interested herself in their perilous occupations, and admired the courage which never failed them. For herself she had no apprehension of death, yet at first her Lowland nature would shudder at the feats which these daring cragsmen took as matters of course. Their fowling expeditions were her parties of pleasure; yet, in spite of herself, her head would turn dizzy as she looked down over the verge of the beetling precipices at the surges breaking far below with no strip of beach between. It was the realizing of the poet's dream of Shakspeare's Cliff, where the huge robber gulls were dwarfed to petrels as they swooped upon their smaller fellows diminished to sea-snipe. Yet the cragsmen went as coolly over the cliff as if they were field labourers stepping down the ladder from a hayrick, though their lives were literally suspended to frayed threads, for the rope which lent them wings was so spliced and time-worn that it seemed as if it must snap with any unusual strain; and sometimes, as he was being lowered from shelf to shelf, the fowler was swinging to and fro like a pendulum, though with no measured beat, but with violent oscillations. Such as it was, that frail rope was a security, but when the cragsman detached himself he had nothing to rely upon, save his firm tread and the clutch of his bare feet. He would tread on some ledge that must be there, though imperceptible from above; and then as she lost sight of him her heart would stand still in sheer sympathy with the desperate adventurer till she saw him reappear. In her unwholesome frame of mind she took a strange delight in these games where her neighbours were gambling with death, and all for a few miserable sea-birds. Once she thrilled with wild satisfaction when she witnessed an accident,—to her subsequent remorse, for she really grieved for the fate of the victim, and came to the help of the widow and orphans.

She had repeatedly admired the man's courage and dexterity. She had followed to see him descend a scaur which was certainly the most dangerous in the island, and consequently a favourite breeding place of the fowl. So dangerous was it that it was seldom ventured upon; but the spring harvest of feathers and oil had been bad, and men must live even if they may die. Lachlan faced the deadly risk with full knowledge and pious stoicism. Had there been a priest he would have shriven himself for the enterprise, for he was a Catholic; as it was, he muttered a credo and a pater or two, and then seriously addressed himself to the work. The chief peril was in overhanging and projecting rocks that cut the strands as the rope ran over them. So the islanders hazarded far more than the life of an individual, and Lachlan was well assured that they would take every possible precaution. All had gone prosperously and the reward was rich. Lachlan had trodden ledges where the hill goats would hardly have found a footing, and stepped lightly from projection to projection where the sea-fowl could scarcely have found a perch. The sea-fowl, lulled by impunity into fatal security, had been noosed and strangled by scores. And now he was to be hauled up with his heavy burden of spoils. Some of the old men shook their heads, but the general feeling was to haul away and get it over. The sooner they were all out of suspense—Lachlan included—the better. He had already been hauled so high that they could see the sweat-drops streaming on his forehead, when the rope hitched in a cleft. It would neither come nor yield, and there Lachlan swung in mid-air with thirteen stone of dead weight fretting it on a blunted knife-edge. The experienced fowler knew his fate. His features were warped with bodily strain and mental anguish as he still clung fast for dear life. Well he knew that the agony must be long drawn out, for he was seated snugly enough in a loop. He could see the horror in the eyes of his wife, who was only prevented from throwing herself over by the hands that held her. He could even hear her wild screams piercing the clamour of the sea-birds. Even his strong, dull brain must have given way, as he spun round in the air beyond the rock his staff could not reach ; but mercifully the inevitable end came more abruptly than he had anticipated. The rope snapped—the bold fowler fell back in space ; and the eyes that followed the fall saw something like a coat in a cloud of feathers disappear in the spray of the breakers.

"It's a good man gone like his father ; and it was the best of the two tows, and God knows where we will get another," ejaculated a grey-haired patriarch, and that in the meantime was poor Lachlan's dirge.

Such dramatic catastrophes were few and far between, but danger in one form or another was ever present. The fishing-boats would put to sea even when the weather-wise little liked the look of the heavens to windward. Over-prudence meant privations or starvation. Then wild weather would blow up, the skies would be leaden and the seas would be seething.. As the wind roared and howled round the rigging of the huts, wives and daughters lay awake, praying and quaking. The belated morning broke in sullen dimness, and anxiety grew into agony as the day drew to a close. Some of the boats had made the shore and been beached and drawn up with infinite peril by chains of men and women who were swept off their legs; but one or more would be missing. Had they gone straight to the bottom, or were they driving before the storm? The wives would wait and watch, and after delaying till hope had died out, resign themselves to mourn the lost. Then some fine morning a sail would be descried in the offing, or the flashes of foam from the oars would be caught in the sunshine. There would be warm embraces and a welcome that was boisterous, or in some cases with feelings too deep for expression. But meantime all the horrors of suspense had been endured, the cup of bitterness had been drained to the very dregs; and who could answer for the morrow, when all that misery might recommence? The sense of an irresistible fatality did much to support them, but the anxieties were abiding while the relief was forgotten.

Lady Grange envied their sensibility, such as it was. At least these prematurely aged crones and care-worn matrons were in everyday communion with the great human family, and their hearts beat in sympathy to the sorrows of others. At least they had somebody to care for and to miss. As with the ravens and falcons breeding in the cliffs, there were hungry nurslings they were bound to look after, and the death of the bread-winning consort threw double duty on the mate. She envied them the turmoil of hopes and fears, with the pre-occupations that compelled them to exertion, and the effort that wore them out all the faster.

She envied, and yet she had her own experiences of peril; but she knew that her death would bring pleasure to many and sorrow to none. The doubtful weather that might have kept her under cover

tempted her abroad. Muffled in plaid and hood
of homespun she defied the cold, the rain and the
damp. More than once she was surprised in
tremendous thunder-storms, but in these she took
a strange joy, as she was transported out of herself
when she was the centre of the strife of the elements.
She would wilfully neglect unmistakable warnings.
Long before the rolling pall of leaden cloud had
cast its heavy shadow over the island, changing the
bright green of the grass to brown and blackening
the pellucid flow of some hill burn, the sea-fowl
had been winging their flight to their rocks with
dolorous shrieks of alarm. There was a preter-
natural stillness in the air, broken by the damp
and fitful puffs of a sea-breeze. There was an
uncanny rushing sound, with a strong earthy
smell. Then the ear-splitting peals would break
overhead, with no distant mutterings or preliminary
warnings. The vivid flashes from the heavenly
cannonade would have come almost simultaneously
with the roar of the artillery; the floodgates would
open to the shock of the sound and the water would
come down in torrents. The surface of the grassy
steeps would seem to heave and slide, like a blanket

shaken by beaters; then trenches would be torn and the floods would escape, hurrying by the shortest course to the brow of the cliff, tumbling in cascades that were burdened by an occasional landslip. Crouching under some projecting rock, she would watch the blinding flashes which fitfully threw spectral lights over the landscape. Having been soaked and saturated in that magnificent performance, she would wait till the storm had driven over to the east, and the soft gleams of watery sunshine had succeeded the lightning's glare. Then she would find her way home, excited, exhausted, and in unusual spirits.

She gave little heed to the lightnings, though they might blast the rocks within bowshot; but the stealthy fogs were more perilous, as the adder is more to be feared than the wild cat. On one occasion she had an escape which, steeled as she fancied she was against dread of death, reminded her that she had the shrinking which is the instinct of humanity. The day was cloudy, the air was close, and she had dropped asleep over a volume of Shakspeare. When she awoke, she was slow to realize where she was, and fancied she must still be wandering in dreamland. She had gone to sleep in daylight; now it was utter darkness. Of course she soon came to her senses, but her bearings were altogether lost. She had wandered to where she had sat down in abstracted mood and had taken no note of the surroundings. All she knew was that she had passed up a gorge on to a plateau, which shelved to the seaward upon every side. In the highlands generally, the sure clue out of such embarrassment is the burn or rill leading down to the lowlands, though there may be tumbling cataracts in its course. On St. Kilda the short watercourses, that frequently run dry, were like so many gutters on a house-roof. If they flowed at all, they might take a plunge of many hundred feet. She went forward, groping her way with outstretched hands; and even in the darkness of a familiar bedroom you may run up against the wardrobe when aiming at the toilette table. More than once she was turned back by a parapet of rock. Frequently she slipped on the damp turf and fell, and with each of these accidents she felt more and more confused. In the darkness and the sense of oppressive solitude, her heart beat so fast as to stop her breath, and her trembling limbs threatened to fail her. Still, out of the mist she heard the subdued and melancholy plaints of the gulls and cormorants. Then a waft of air fanned her cheek, and a spectral form swept over her shoulder. With a scream the great white-tailed eagle rose swiftly and vanished, for the wild bird of the hill and ocean was more startled than herself.

With hands still outstretched she plodded onward, knowing that she had taken little measure of the distance, but marvelling to find so much of level ground. Then she stumbled again, and as she fell forward she wondered at a damp rush of air that struck sharply under her chin. She crept onwards a foot or so and felt again; but her hands were groping in empty space, and when she let her arms go down, they met no resistance. Her heart stopped beating for some moments, and the cold perspiration poured from her burning brow. She lent an ear to listen and, reverberating upwards from unknown depths, she heard the sullen murmur of the never silent surge. She swooned, and how long she lay senseless she knew not. When she came to herself again the mists had gone, her head was pillowed on the heather tufts that fringed the precipice, and within half-a-dozen yards a venerable raven was examining her gloatingly out of half-closed eyes. Had the swoon lasted but a few minutes more, he would have been busy over his business as undertaker.

The effects of that adventure shook her for a day or two, and sent her to bed, but she was to have another which had a more abiding influence on her fortunes. In fact it proved the happy turning-point of that troubled career. It has been said that a "stickit minister" turned missionary and catechist was the only soul on the rock—save one—with whom she could hold intercourse in the Southland speech, or who had ideas in common with her own. After her first transports of grief and despair had calmed down, she had naturally been not disinclined to make friends with the man. Had he had the rudiments of tact, or any glimmerings of delicacy, she might have been won over to unbosom herself, and the catechist might have become her helpful father confessor. But though excellent and even saintly according

to his lights, he was zealous to fanaticism, narrow-minded and obtrusive.   He forced himself
prematurely on her privacy, he abounded in exhortations which were summarily cut short, and he
fretted that haughty spirit into intense antipathy,
the rather that he obviously smarted for the lady's
contempt.   When Satan was strong with her, she
took a malicious pleasure in seeking him out that
she might ostentatiously shun him.   So that the
catechist came to detest the captive so far as a
Christian abounding in charity might conscientiously
hate.   In fact his conscience began to reproach
him for lack of charity, till he came to hate her
more and more.

But Mr. McAlpine had one fair daughter, and
she was far from sharing his feelings.   Jessie was
a soft-hearted and romantic girl of nineteen, and
the fate of this high-born and unfortunate lady
appealed intensely to her sympathies.   Novels
were scarce then—Jessie had never read one in
her life; but here was the tragic sublimity of
sensational romance in full action under her eyes.
Her father had laid his commands on her to hold
aloof, and she never dreamed of disobeying.   But

as she knitted or spun, or dreamed over the needles
of an evening, she wove many a scheme in that
pretty head of hers, in which she broke the spider's
web and helped the prisoner to freedom. MacLeod
might give behests to his clan, but he was no
chieftain of hers. Her father spoke mysteriously
of horrors and scandals unfit for her ears, and
so her curiosity was piqued and kept alive. He
warned her against contamination, though to her
purity all things were pure. But even if her father
had been otherwise minded, the lady scarce deigned
to see her, and that was the worst. The truth
was that Lady Grange, being at feud with the
catechist, was more than disposed to visit the
faults of the father on his remarkably attractive
child. Jessie's fresh bloom and innocent beauty
were causes of perpetual offence to the *blasée* and
worn woman of the world, who had been stained
by sin and hardened by suffering. So that the
shy and wistfully sympathetic glances had ever
met with chilling contempt.

Jessie was not only indefatigable in spinning as
Penelope, though she got over the woofs at a very
different pace, but she had a taste for botany, which

o

her father encouraged. She had sat at the feet of the old herbalists of St. Kilda, but her researches had given her teachers new lights as to medicinal plants and precious simples. So her rambles about the rifts and the cliffs had an object, for there were sovereign herbs that were seldom met with growing capriciously, and generally in awkward situations. But Jessie was sure-footed as any goat, and she tripped along ledges between the wind and the water as lightly as any fairy footing it on the greensward. Lady Grange had a good head of her own, and with custom and stoical indifference, now she seldom experienced the sense of dizziness. But she weighed rather heavier than she cared to think of; her years had been stiffening the sinews which once carried her so lightly through the minuet, and she envied the fearlessness of the lithesome mountain maid. Whether it were envy or not, or whatever the reason, Jessie, whom she never seemed to see, was the object that interested her most on St. Kilda, and she had got into the way of following her at a distance in her rambles.

One day the girl bent her steps towards the edge of the Scaur of Rusk, a beetling precipice which

even the boldest fowlers were inclined to avoid.
After descending steeply for some score of fathoms,
it actually curved inwards, before it sunk sheer to
the billows. The girl was evidently in search of
something, and knew where to seek. Going upon
her knees she crawled to the brink and peered cautiously over. She seemed to hesitate; then she took
her resolution, slipped over, and disappeared. The
older woman involuntarily pressed a hand on her
heart; then in anxiety and excitement she hurried
down to the cliff. When she ventured to the edge
to peep over in turn, she almost believed the girl
would be gone, though her careful but easy move-
ments suggested nothing like suicide. No; there she
was, on a mere scrap of shelving stone, stooping
and plucking at a plant that had struck root in
one of the crevices. Thrusting it into her bosom
to leave both hands at liberty, she turned as com-
posedly to reascend as if she had been climbing
a ladder to a hay-loft. At the second step, as she
reached out to lay hold of a projection, the stone
gave way between her fingers, and there was a
tiny gravel-slip. It was nothing more than might
have filled a good-sized coal-scuttle, nevertheless it

opened an impracticable chasm. The path was barred as effectually as if it had been crossed by a yawning gulf. In a moment the young rock-climber realized the situation. She knew well it was the standing rule on the islet never to go fowling except at least in pairs. She knew there was nothing for it but to resign herself, for any effort was hopeless. Her only chance was to cry for help, and that was a desperate one; the shrill scream, which would have carried far in a calm like a fog-whistle, was drowned between the clamour of resentful sea-fowl and the roar of the surge below. Though her heart was good, and her nerves were steeled by habit, she dared not glance down to those distant breakers. She looked upwards, ceased to struggle or to cry, and breathed a prayer that she might have grace and strength to endure without murmuring, a slow and horribly lingering death. Even when her father and the neighbours should arrange a search, she was out of sight and they had no clue to her track. And searches were seldom persevered with on St. Kilda, for a slip and a fatal catastrophe were the natural explanations of a disappearance.

She little suspected that she was being watched all the time. Lady Grange, lying flat on her chest, had been near enough to trace the passage of each rapid emotion on the sufferer's features. And never, perhaps, had she envied her more than when Jessie resigned herself to the death which might be slow, but was apparently inevitable. There were three courses before her ladyship. She might hurry back to summon assistance; she might walk away and keep her own counsel; or she might risk her life in an attempt at rescue. The fiend who was ever at her elbow whispered to her to take the middle course. She was actually rising to be gone when selfishness saved her: she dare not burden herself with a new weight of remorse. So she hastened to the rescue, when, if she had hesitated, she must have held back. Scarcely conscious how she had done it, she was standing on the upper edge of the slip, and stretching down her hand. There was a swimming in her eyes, and a singing in her ears, when she pulled herself together to steady herself on her feet; but she had resolution enough to avert her eyes from the abyss. Had Jessie snatched at the hand she must have lost her footing; but the girl was perfectly calm, and laid hold of her wrist without a tremor. The support, slight as it was, was sufficient: it gave the indispensable *point d'appui*. A few seconds more and Lady Grange was safely fainting on the turf, while Jessie was hurrying to a spring to fill her head-gear with water.

Snatched from death by something like a miracle, Jessie was guilty of disobedience. Perhaps for the first time in her life she forgot her father's commands. Naturally shy, and holding the strange lady in awe, she was not effusive of thanks. But her soft hazel eyes spoke for her, and when Lady Grange came back to consciousness, she met their wistful, pleading expression, and felt theirsilent reproach. Had it been Jessie who had saved herself, she would probably have hardened her heart; but now she was surprised into unwonted tenderness. The girl who was helping her was a thing of her own—the living symbol of one generous and disinterested action. She clasped her in her arms, pressed a passionate kiss on her lips, and so far committed she could not draw back. The barriers between them were broken down. The captive, apparently abandoned by God and man, had made a friend, and found a *protegée :* the girl felt that the devotion of a lifetime would be too little to repay the life she had received.

She went home to the paternal hovel in no slight anxiety, though with a mind made up. The lively sense of gratitude outweighed all other considerations. Yet she looked forward to a stormy interview, and probably a renewal of orders she would feel bound to disobey, for well she knew her father's dour disposition. But she had underrated the parental tenderness of the taciturn, self-contained man. As she told her tale, and acted the scene with dramatic realism, McAlpine's breath came short and quick. When she had done, the catechist heaved a tremendous sigh, like the wind escaping from a burst bellows. It was as if he himself had just escaped some deadly peril. Then he trod delicately across the earthen floor to the cupboard, where he took a long pull at a whisky bottle—an indulgence which, to do him justice, he rarely permitted himself—then with cheeks and lips that had revived their colour, he came back to clasp his daughter in his arms. It was the second time she had been embraced within an hour or two, and the last occasion had been on her eighteenth birthday. McAlpine was as little demonstrative as Lady Grange. But he was a man of decision, though ill to move, and when he did speak it was to the purpose.

"Jessie, my lass, we must do something for that woman."

"I was thinking so myself, father," Jessie managed to stammer out, in equal delight and astonishment.

"There must be good in her yet, for all they may say to the contrary; but were she waur than Jezebel, or—or—the witch o' Endor, we must see what she would want, and seek to give her a helping hand. Aye, even if we had to find work on the mainland—and 'deed I've been many a time thinking o' that, for I'm wearying o' this Patmos, where the seed is scattered upon the rock, among the fowls and the Romans."

CHAPTER XIV.

A DELIVERY BY PARCEL POST.

An old Highland dame was keeping house, with her cat, in a garret among the chimney-stacks of the Cówgate in Auld Reekie. She lived and sometimes starved on the small savings she had put together in long service, and now and again, from charity, for though the old lady was proud, she accepted some charitable help from her minister. The only sensation which broke the dull monotony of her existence was the rare receipt of a parcel from St. Kilda. The catechist was her nephew, and she was glad that he should keep her in mind; as for her grandniece, she had never seen the girl, but she was gratified by her kindly letters and thoughtful little love-tokens. She felt she could love her dearly, and she would have liked well to embrace her with a blessing before she took her departure.

One morning the old lady's spirits had been at

low water-mark, and she had been seeking for comfort
in the pages of the well-thumbed Bible. Never had
she felt more drearily that she had nothing to live
for; never had she indulged in more longing desires
for a peaceful flitting to the Grey Friars kirkyard.
There came a heavy step on the dark stairs, and a
rapping at the door. She opened to a Highland
cadie with a weather-stained and carefully corded
package, and she knew well from whence it came.
The old lady brightened up wonderfully, though
she emptied the corner of the money drawer for
carriage and porterage. Comfort had come, almost
miraculously, when she least expected it, and she
bitterly reproached herself for blasphemous mur-
murings. She would have dallied with her pleasure
in unknotting the string with trembling fingers,
and she regretted that she was forced to fall back
on the scissors. The contents delighted her, and
she loved the unknown grandniece more than ever
for the thoughtful consideration which had animated the busy fingers. There were warm stockings
and mittens, but above all, one of those delightful
veils, best of protections against the bitter winds
from the Firth, which have since become fashion-

able under the designation of "Shetlands." There
was the customary short and affectionate letter,
but reverting to the veil, the strange thing was
that there was a great rent across it. That was
not like Jessie. Moreover, it was impossible for
the self-respecting old dame to go forth with such a
kenspeckle object while it was torn. But doubtless
the parcel had been made up in haste, and the
lassie was considerate as ever. For there was a
ball of the homespun wool, evidently meant to
repair the damage. Old Elspeth McAlpine went
to work at once, but the wool was oddly broken
and entangled, and so she proceeded to unwind it.
It was rolled around a piece of written paper, stuck
full of pins as a pincushion. Of course such
treasures as "the preens" were not to be wasted,
and she carefully drew them out. Then she came
to the kernel, in the shape of a tightly twisted
note, secured with a wafer and duly addressed,
although not to her. Sorely mystified, Elspeth
put on her spectacles, and turned at last to the
"hand o' write" on the outer paper for an explanation. The writing was that of her grandniece.

"In the name of God I beseech you to lose no

time in carrying the letter that goes herewith to
Mr. Monypenny, the Writer to the Signet. There
are life and death depending on it, and he knows
what must be done."

To say that Elspeth was dumfounded would be
putting the matter mildly. The mystery of the
communication and the romance of the commission
might well have staggered a stronger brain, and
made a man versed in the ways of the world to
pause and hesitate. But Elspeth was a simple old
wife, absolutely devoid of imagination. She never
troubled to stop and think; the injunction was
peremptory, and the path of duty was plain, if dark.
She donned her most decent clothes, wrapped the
veil round her face, torn as it was, and set forth on
her walk to the office of Mr. Monypenny.

After long waiting in the antechamber, in company of a silent clerk, she was admitted to an
audience. The lawyer's reception was chilling,
and indeed he was only eager to get rid of her.
However, when she had told her tale, his curiosity
was naturally excited. He stepped to the window,
for the light was failing, opened the missive, and
glanced his eyes over it. Then Elspeth, if she was

gratified by sensations, might have been satisfied by the effect she had produced. Monypenny stared at her as if she had come from the other world, read again and with the closest attention, and rubbed his eyes as if he misdoubted them.

"You say you ken no more of this business than that you have told," he ejaculated at last, though rather thinking aloud than questioning.

"So I said, sir," answered Elspeth dryly, for she was offended by the implied doubt.

He scarcely heard her. In fact, if the message from St. Kilda had dumfounded old Elspeth, the lawyer was thrown off his balance altogether. Otherwise, after vague questioning as to the credibility of the catechist and his daughter, he would never, with some confused hope of getting light on the subject, have read his letter aloud. His carelessness, as he realized too late, compromised himself and his course of action. For Elspeth, though unimaginative as her old tabby cat, had still the curiosity of a woman, and as she listened, the pith of the momentous despatch was indelibly impressed on a retentive memory, schooled in committing the Scriptures to heart. It was from Lady Grange. It told briefly, but forcibly, the story of the violent abduction and the prolonged seclusion; it said that he as family lawyer was naturally the party to whom she had hoped and longed to appeal; and it charged him as a man of character, a man of business and a Christian, not to lose an hour in bringing her case before the officers of the Crown. "I have waited and watched for years," she wrote, "for this chance of making myself heard from my living tomb, and it may well be that I will never have another opportunity. I solemnly charge you, on soul and conscience, as you shall answer to God at the great Day of Judgment, to plead the cause of the captive and to break her chains, for the enemy and oppressors are cruel and powerful."

"That's just it," ejaculated the poor man, in great tribulation. "Powerful they are and cruel; it's ill meddling with Grange leagued with Lovat. I care little for MacLeod—it's a far cry to Dunvegan. But Lovat and Grange! To think that yon woman's living yet!—and why the deevil need she have turned to me of all folk to bind sic a burden on my conscience as that?"

Yet he knew that her reasons for turning to him

were obvious enough.   For long he had been the
confidential lawyer of the Erskines, and had drawn
up such settlements as had been made when
Rachel Chiesley wedded James Erskine.   His credit
stood high among leading Writers to the Signet,
and he was known for a douce, respectable church-
goer, whose word was believed as good as his bond.
So it was, in fact, and he would have been the last
man under ordinary circumstances to connive at a
flagrant breach of the laws.   But he had never been
strong of will or seriously tempted, and now that
he was ageing he was enamoured of ease.   Making
trouble in this matter was like handling a hedgehog
or plunging *in puris naturalibus* into the heart of a
whin thicket.

After all, it was perhaps well for him that he
had read the letter aloud and let the sound-hearted
Highlandwoman into the secret.   Left to himself his
timidity and the spirit of self-indulgence might have
sought to soothe his conscience with such sophis-
tries as had made Grange the most miserable and
remorseful of men.   He would have temporized and
gained leisure to reflect, and for that, indeed, the
habits of legal procrastination would have been

very sufficient justification. But the spirit of
Elspeth was roused—her warmest sympathies were
excited, and she would stand no sort of nonsense
and hear of no delay. The woman's fixed resolution
asserted its ascendancy. At last she fairly lost
patience and broke forth :

"I wonder to hear you, sir. It's weel for you to
sit at ease in your elbow-chair, and speak peaceably
of moving warily and cannily. I wonder would
ye be as patient, if you had been misguided like
yon poor lady, who is wearing out the wearisome
days and waiting for a reply, all the time that you
and me are havering here. It's different for the
like o' her frae they folk o' mine. She was brought
up in kings' palaces and clad in soft raiment, and
cothered upon sunkets ; and now, for aught we ken,
she's clothed in the feathers of the sea-fowl and
feeding upon their stinking flesh. But eneuch said ;
if ye will not seek out the Lord Advocate, I will.
Maybe it's ower late the day, but I will be wi' him
the first thing in the morning, though I should not
have a wink o' sleep. So I'll be wishing you good
day, and if there's justice in the land, he'll be seeking
after you before the sun goes down on the morrow."

Having delivered her ultimatum, Elspeth rose to go, but the lawyer arrested her. A pitiable figure of irresolution, he was like a nervous horseman craning at an ugly fence, but he was forced to throw his heart over and drive home the spurs. With such dignity as he could assume at short notice, he hastened to assure his visitor that all should be done as she desired.

Elspeth looked him straight in the eyes and seemed to be satisfied.

" See that it be so, then, sir, and I wish you well through the business, for it maun be managed somehow, either by you or me."

Worked up by indignation and unlooked-for opposition, the quiet, humble old woman scarcely knew herself, as she walked down the darksome stairs she had ascended with bashful breathlessness. Her apprehensions of Mr. Monypenny had changed to something like contempt, but in any case, and come what might, she would keep him up to the mark.

And Monypenny, who had learned a good deal of human nature, was fully assured of that. So much so, that he bestirred himself, lest Elspeth

P

should be before him, and accosted the Advocate in the Parliament House on the very next morning.

At last, and in spite of the law's delays and difficulties in the Scotland of the day, a gleam of light seemed to be breaking on the unfortunate captive. But it was her destiny to be dogged by persistent mischances. Monypenny had been startled out of his ordinary prudence. Instead of speaking softly and deliberately, as was his wont, the stormy interview with Elspeth had excited him. The matter that he would have desired to keep secret, in the meantime, had been discussed in the shrillest of tones. He had quite forgotten that doors have ears and keyholes. The confidential clerk in the outer chamber had not. He was naturally of an enquiring disposition, as it behoved him to be; he bent his head and lent his ears and listened with all his might. When he ushered the old lady out, he knew nearly as much of the business as either she or Monypenny. Necessarily his first thought was how he might use the involuntary confidence to the best advantage for himself. Nor was the decision difficult in the circumstances. Monypenny might have been more cautious had he remembered how the clerk came recommended. He had been taken into the office of the family lawyer at the request of Lord Grange, though his lordship, who dreaded the suspicion of being kept in leading strings, had not cared to mention that he was really the *protégé* of Lovat. As matter of fact, the man knew well to whom he was indebted, and on whom he must depend for obstruction or advancement. Lovat never missed a chance; he never gave anything for nothing; he had a memory for all whom he had in any way befriended, and looked for their services in return. If they broke the implied bargain, so much the worse for them.

Had Lovat been in the North or beyond his reach, he might have hesitated as to his course. In any case he would have turned his discovery to account. But he might have intimated to his master that the awkward secret was in his keeping, or he might have gone to Grange, as the party most directly concerned, and as Lovat's friend and confidant. As it chanced, however, Lovat was in his Edinburgh lodgings; only that morning the clerk had made one of the disreputable tail who smoked and gossiped at the head of the close. Accordingly, when office hours were over, thither he repaired again, as in duty bound.

The news he carried was startling, and his lordship received it characteristically. He had dined early, and the good liquor was dying out in him now the supper hour was drawing on. He burst out in a tempest of execration on the unlucky visitor; he damned the lady at large for all the vexation she was giving him, and he doubly cursed James Erskine, whose fearsome nature was at the bottom of all the trouble. Then, as the peril was urgent, he swallowed a glass of brandy and coolly buckled to business. He invoked the help of no amanuensis. Though the bother of the thing went sorely against the grain, from a muddy standish, with the worn stump of a quill, he indited a missive. It was full of Christian charity and high-flown sentiment, for, as he said to himself, "If the alarm be given and they send riders along the roads, there is no saying into whose hands it may be delivered." It took a cursory view of Scottish politics, and mentioned incidentally that word had come, though vaguely, of the death of that unhappy mad woman, the Lady Grange. "Though it is a sad satisfaction to be assured that she had all the care and tenderness of which her melancholy condition admitted. And, yet, it may not be true, for these lunatic folk live long!" There was a good deal interspersed which the correspondent for whom it was intended might understand, but which could scarcely be misconstrued by Government to the writer's serious disadvantage. There was a postscript—"If you need to hear more, you may speer for news at the bearer." The letter was sealed and formally superscribed, "To my very Honourable Kinsman, the Macleod of Macleod."

Then he summoned one of his trusted gentlemen henchmen who had been bidden to have all in readiness for a long journey, though nothing had been said as to the destination. The chieftain bent a frowning glance on him from under his shaggy eyebrows. Then, when he saw the stout Duihnewassel shrink and tremble, he changed his countenance and smiled good-humouredly.

"Toss off that cup, man, to a safe and swift ride and a happy delivery. You have supped well and your horse is ready saddled?"

The other merely bowed and waited.

" To the saddle then, and spare neither spur nor horseflesh till you have put the passes behind you. Ye know the places where you can shift the steed. Once ayont the corries of the Blackmount you are safe, but waste no time on the road, and grudge neither breath nor boot-leather, as you ever hope for good at my hands, till you give the letter to MacLeod. And hearken here—and print the message on your memory. It will go ill with you, my man, if you forget a word, for the credit, and may be the life, of more than one is depending on it." More cautious than Mr. Monypenny, he muttered the important message, and emphatically repeated it. " You have it now. Lock it fast till you come to Dunvegan, and should any mischance befall, which God forbid, see that neither threat nor torture force it from you. ' A nod's as good as a wink,' my friend." So, with a very significant nod indeed, and an unctuous " God-speed ye," which resounded down the stairs, the lord of Lovat dismissed his envoy.

In promptly acting without communicating with Grange, Lovat showed his usual sagacity. He wisely decided for his friend without preliminary consultation, and as the stronger will invariably prevailed, it came to the same in the end. As for Monypenny, though he had been driven by the stout old Highland dame to take a formidable leap, on reflection he did not regret the hasty promise. In his professional way he was a worthy man, and could scarcely have been easy had he not taken action in the matter. Then he remembered who the Advocate was. Erskine of Tinwald was a not very distant kinsman of Lord Mar, to whose patronage he was indebted for his first advancement. At the same time, and since the disastrous rising of the '15, he had been zealous for Government to fining, imprisoning, and banishing the disaffected. He had made himself many enemies by his activity in baffling Jacobite machinations. Yet he had never ceased to be on friendly terms with his good cousin, the Lord Grange. If Monypenny shifted the responsibility on him, he would act as seemed best to him ; probably the Advocate would steer a middle course, and seek to do justice to the wife without bearing hard upon the husband. That was for him to consider. Then the family lawyer could smooth things over with his client, by declaring that nothing else could possibly have been done, and that it was for Grange to use his influence with the chief law officer of the Crown.

Yet it was with no little nervousness that he sought the interview with Grange. He discreetly waited till after the dinner-hour, but he timed his visit so that his lordship should be fortified rather than fuddled. With similar caution he had measured his own drink, although he braced himself with an extra glass or two.

The unsuspicious Grange received him hilariously. He knew of nothing likely to give him trouble.

"Ay! George, and what brings you here at this unwonted hour. A sight of you is good for sore eyes. Is it that some clerk o' the Session has slipped off his stool, and that you want me to give you a lift with the President? Well, well, Duncan is my very good friend. But never heed your errand, in the meantime, man, the matter will keep; step ben, and sit down and fill up your glass."

Monypenny, with the jovial welcome, felt more ill at ease than he had feared. He filled his glass mechanically, and looked Grange silently in the face. The old lawyer saw at once there was something wrong. The Nemesis that was ever haunting him cast a darker shadow than usual over his shoulder. His look grew hard and his tone changed. In ten seconds he seemed ten years older than before.

"Out with it, man! Come to the point! What are you feared for, that you keep hanging in the wind? Are you trimming your sails for a breeze from the Western Isles?"

The query compromised him in no way, for though all the world was awake to Jacobite intrigue, surely Monypenny could know nothing of St. Kilda.

"I see your lordship gathers the purport of my call."

Grange got up and paced the room in agitation he did not seek to conceal. The tomb, then, had given up the living dead, and judgment had fallen upon him with accumulated arrears of interest. He had a dark glimpse into the blackest of possible futures, peopled by all the phantoms of guilt and remorse; but the present was what immediately concerned him. His fair reputation would be blasted in a day; he would be a scandal in the Churches, and a laughing-stock to the scoffers. Even if he escaped actual conviction for a grave offence, his tolerant brethren of the Bench would cold-shoulder him, and the Judge who had once presided over the criminal tribunal would be the jest of the briefless in the Outer House. The tables to be turned on the veteran intriguer who had been found out! Possibly the Lord Justice Clerk in the dock, between a couple of the city guard! His imagination pictured his successor, who had no love for him, pronouncing sentence and solemnly advising him to repent and make his peace with an offended God, amid the sneers of the Court and the laughter of the galleries. But, at least, it would be well to know the worst.

He controlled himself with an effort, threw himself back in his chair, and signed to Monypenny to speak.

"How did it all come about? Make a clean breast of it, man."

Then the lawyer told the story, honestly enough. All he did was to shift the responsibility from himself, and prove that he was inevitably a passive

instrument. At the same time, having the whip-
hand of his lordship, he disavowed any idea of
becoming accomplice in a crime, and so his
explanation was somewhat contradictory.

"That auld Highland witch must bear all the
wyte. I assure your lordship she spoke like one
inspired, and in her passion for what she called
pity and justice, she was neither to hold nor bind.
Yet, I'm bound to say, and between ourselves, she
was no that far wrong. If wrong has been done
—now it has come to light—the wrong must be
speedily righted. Surely you must see that, and
I know few that are better fitted than yourself, my
lord, to manage what, at the best, is a queer piece
of business."

"All very well," said Grange, not insensible to
the compliment, "but how came you to go straight
to the Advocate?"

"It was the only thing I could do to satisfy the
wife, and besides, it was the best thing for your
lordship. I have spared you a kittle bit of work,
and I said, moreover, to Tinwald, that, like all the
world, I was well assured of the rectitude of your
conduct."

"But the funeral, man, and the mad devilry of
the mourning and the weepers, and the many
condolences I got for the departed!"

"Aye! that was a mischancy ploy; but what's
done cannot be undone, and we must do our best
to mend it. If your lady was in a condition
demanding sequestration, it was incumbent on you
to save the honour of your noble House. I always
surmised I saw the hand of Lovat in that, but with
all his auld-world craft, Simon Fraser and his
wiles are apt to overreach themselves."

"D—n Simon Fraser!" said Grange, heartily,
"that I should say so. He has led me deep into the
wood, but I fear it passes his wit to take me out
of it again."

"I know not that," answered Monypenny,
meditatively. "To give the deil his due, if he's
for ever in trouble, he has not his match in Britain
for slipping out of the snares. It's the guile and
the venom as well of the old serpent. And, mind
you this, my lord, I might have scrupled to go so
speedily to the Advocate, had he not been your
very good friend. Then there's the Lord President.
Duncan Forbes is an honourable gentleman and

an upright judge; but for yourself, you've always been friendly eneuch with him, and I know not how, but that uncanny neighbour of his, Lovat, has always had more to say with Culloden than was beseeming. If you play your cards, as you can, you may anyway draw the straws over the eyes of the authorities. It is not for me to proffer advice, but this I maun say, in the words of Scripture, 'What thou doest, do quickly.' You lose credit for good-will to make reparation for any error of judgment, with each precious minute you put off."

That was entirely Grange's opinion, but to see the Advocate without previously communicating with Lovat was not to be thought of. Not only did he trust to the counsel of Achitophel, but though he would not own as much to himself, he dared not act independently.

As he put it, " Simon's over boots and hose in the affair, and it would hardly be right or honest not to take him along with me."

In all his trouble, besides, he felt a certain satisfaction in having, for once, the earliest intelligence and taking his all-knowing friend by surprise.

"I shall like to see his face when I tell him the grease is in the fire."

He soon had satisfaction on that score. Lovat received him with a quizzical smile on his wrinkled features, and his withered jaws looked more like a pair of nut-crackers than usual.

"Well, James, what are you thinking of it?" was all he said, and Grange was so taken aback by this new proof of his dangerous confederate's omniscience that he was struck speechless.

Lovat leered satirically, and repeated the advice of Monypenny. "I'm thinking that the sooner you have a word yourself with the Advocate, the better. However," he went on, "you were right to come here first. It's always well to know the lie of the land before you go groping in a fog."

"I always thought you were near o' kin to the Fiend, Simon, and now I'm convinced of it. How, in the name of heaven, or the other place, did you get wind——"

"Never you heed, James, how I got wind of it. The winds are aye bringing news to my lugs from all the airts of Scotland." Nor could all Grange's anxious enquiries persuade him to further explanation. It was his principle never to betray a spy—unless it suited him—and his practice to envelop himself as much as possible in an impenetrable atmosphere of mysterious omniscience.

"I must needs say, my lord—" began Grange, hotly.

"I know what you would say, James, and there might be, as it were a fashion of justice in it. But you need not 'my lord' me. My word is passed to tell nothing of my informants, and you would not tempt me to break it. With them, as with others we could name, their heads would be in jeopardy were I in the habit of coming out with an unconsidered word," and he looked at his friend with much significance. "Anyhow, James, believe me, that it is best for you that you should know as little as possible now. There's no gainsaying that there's an ill bit of steering to be done; suffice it for you to be assured that the helm is in safe hands. Hearken to me. Seek the Advocate after supper. Say that you know him for a righteous judge in Israel, who is not to be swayed from his duty by a hairbreadth, for fear or favour. Mind you stick to that, for the words will suit you well, and your kinsman and namesake is like yourself, and likes to be well kittled. Say nothing about the kinship, and little of the honour of the Erskines : he'll mind upon that himself, when he has the time to think. You can hint to him, with a bye-word though, that you were in sore distress what to do for the credit of the family with a woman with a crazy brain—the true daughter of Dalry—mind you mention that—who was like to make a notorious public scandal. Say it was hell never to lay your head on your pillow, with the sure knowledge she meant to do you a mischief, without the thought that you might waken in the other world, and that, to excite the shame and scorn of malevolent illwishers, you were minded to put her away privily. But what signifies prompting and preaching to you ? You can say all that need be said far better than me. Only remember that she has been tended with all observance and tenderness, and that it was out of the love and affection you bore her, that she was sent to an honourable exile in the North. With the Bedlam bodies in the South, her lot would have been misery, cages, and chains, with recovery out of the question. Sequestrated in the caller air of the Highlands, with the hills of heather for the walls, and the waves for bolts and bars, you could always console yourself with the hope of restoration."

"She will have her own tale to tell, when they find her," answered Grange, gloomily.

"Doubtless, when they do find her," rejoined Lovat, dryly. "My measures are always taken bytimes, man; and you may trust me that everything is well cared for."

"You do not mean——?"

"Not a whit, man? I mean nothing. For me, she may die of age or sorrow. Now that the Advocate and Duncan Forbes are on the track, I would be the last to harm a hair of her head. But one thing I dare to predict: they may be good seekers, but they'll be ill-finders. Were it worth while, there should never one of their messengers get beyond Glencoe, but natheless, the messages of the Crown shall have safe dispatch to the Long Island, and, if need be, to St. Kilda. And that minds me that while you proffer every assistance to the Advocate, I must possess my good gossip Culloden with the true state of the case."

Nor could his lordship be induced to say another

word. He pleasantly hustled Grange out of the room, bidding him sup and drink in moderation to prepare himself for the interview with the Advocate. When that critical interview was over, Grange was considerably reassured. His craft could take the form of candid simplicity, and few men could be more plausibly persuasive when it pleased him. The Advocate, who was the soul of honour and integrity, had at first, when they foregathered, been courteously distant. Before they parted, having disposed of three bottles of Bordeaux, they were conversing lightly on indifferent subjects. Even the awkward farce of the funeral had been smoothed over. Doubtless it was his duty to have Lady Grange brought to Edinburgh, that her state might be reported upon by capable physicians. She had made deliberate appeal to the judgment seat of Cæsar, and if she had been wronged, the law must right her. In short, it came to this, that he would do his duty, but all his sympathies were with the unfortunate husband, and the poor lady, who was sighing out her soul on the lonely sea-rock, had found an upright, but singularly lukewarm protector.

CHAPTER XV.

THE CUP AND THE LIP.

MEANTIME there were anxious hearts on St. Kilda. The grateful catechist had been easily won to lend himself to his daughter's device, but, though willing to accept, if need were, the crown of martyrdom, he was, nevertheless, a canny Scot. Though prepared for the worst, for the chiefs whom he offended were all-powerful in these parts, he trusted that his disinterestedness might be rewarded even in this world. As for his daughter, being youthful, buoyant, and inexperienced, she would entertain no doubts at all. Heaven would speed the lines she had penned to their destination, and the fiery trials of the persecuted captive would be ended. Lady Grange, who knew the world of Scotland better, and who had had to bear many a bitter disappointment, would have been less hopeful. But the girl's sanguine spirit, the confidence in the beneficent arrangements of a righteous Providence communicated itself to her—for now the

two were seldom apart—and she began, painfully
and anxiously, to count the days which separated
her from restoration to her former station.   In
somewhat premature gratitude for the impending
release, her temper was marvellously softened.
She almost felt that in return for what seemed
a miraculous salvation, she might be content to
let byegones be byegones.   Jessie, who was con-
stantly at her side as her better angel, combating
the devils of revenge who had possessed her for
so long, though careful not to obtrude her advice,
never missed an occasion for strengthening those
resolutions.   She induced the lady to shorten the
dragging days by accompanying her on charitable visits to the cottagers, or rather to the
hovel-dwellers.   In the exhilarating prospects of
approaching happiness, for all things are relative,
Lady Grange began to take a more earnest and
personal interest in good works than she had done
when a hopeless prisoner in Hesker.   If she could
not speak in their own tongue to the poor, the
sick, and the crippled, she found a sensitive and
eloquent interpreter in her companion.   But the
expression of her fine though careworn countenance

was the most speaking commentary on her soothing
words. Her father solemnly warned Jessie against
being puffed up with carnal pride at having made
so notable a convert. Nevertheless, the old Adam
was always chuckling in himself, and he dreamed
of being transferred by powerful patronage to a
wider sphere of usefulness, when, in decent garments and a comfortable manse, he should preach
the Word with the authority of respectability, and
warn sinners to repentance with all the fervour that
came of sufficient meat and drink.

Nor was he the only one who indulged in the
bright day-dreams which seemed on the eve of
being realized. When the sun was shining, the
lady and her young friend would stretch themselves
on some slope of turf. When the rain was beating
on the roof of the cottage, they would draw their
stools nearer to the peat fire in which the rain-
drops were spattering, and discuss their brightening
prospects. Though Jessie modestly protested, her
ladyship insisted that she should make a lady of
her, "Not but that Nature has done it already,
but you ought to have every advantage of which
circumstances have hitherto deprived you." When

she went on to speak of matrimony and a suitable husband, Jessie blushed suspiciously. She set her pretty lips, and seemed to shake her curls in decisive negation. The older woman suspected much, but on that point she could bring the girl to no confession. "I shall have to provide for some loon of a lover as well as for herself, and a sad pity it is," she thought, regretfully. She little guessed that the girl's heart entanglement was a blessing for which she herself would have reason to be thankful. Repeatedly she approached the delicate subject, like a Highland sheltie testing a quaking bog with his forefeet. She longed to know the truth, but as often as she tried she was warned back by the blushes and the heaving bosom. It was not the least of Jessie's charms, that the transparent skin, if slightly bronzed by the sea-breezes, more sure in its indications than any weather-glass, betrayed her innocent secrets in swift rushes of the tell-tale blood.

The days passed on, and the time arrived when even cool and rational calculations might look for an answer, making due allowance for delays. The weather chanced to be unusually fine and warm,

and those lounges on the brink of some beetling
precipice would be prolonged till the shades of the
falling night were darkening the eastern horizon.
As the critical moment approached, and threatened
to go by, they said less of their hopes, but each
saw that the other, as they talked or worked, was
ever casting wistful looks to seaward. One morning
they were seated in a cosy nook which sheltered
them from the breezes. There was nothing to be
seen over the wide waste of waters but the fulmars
dancing on the crests of the waves, and the gulls
that were floating and swooping between the sky
and the breakers. Suddenly Jessie seized the
lady's wrist—she would never have been guilty of
such familiarity unless surprised into strange
excitement. Lady Grange followed the pointing
of her finger, and saw what seldom was seen by
the islanders twice in a twelvemonth, the sails
of a little vessel rounding the southern headland.
She was making a short stretch out to sea, pre-
paratory to tacking and standing in for the
anchorage. The women threw themselves into
each other's arms, and Lady Grange lifted up her
voice and wept. The relief was so intense that

her gratitude was dumb. The doubts that had always haunted her were dissipated; the long-delayed rescue had come at last, and there were the sails that were to waft her back to civilization. Jessie fell on her knees with streaming eyes, and drew the lady down beside her.

The cutter steered in to the shore, and dropped her anchor, but still they lingered. After the long protracted sufferings, after the many disappointments, the captive dallied delightfully with the joyous announcement awaiting her. Such moments of poignant pleasure as these could never be lived again, and were not to be lightly thrown away. The more practical Jessie recalled her to actualities.

"Aye, the sight of the sails has been like a blink o' paradise to you; but see, madam, the folk from the clachan are stirring, and they will be seeking us."

So they got up to descend the hill. Ere they slipped down the first declivity, Lady Grange paused and looked back.

"Never can I forget that blessed nook, yet I would fain fix each stone and ilka blade of grass in my memory. There was a time when I cursed this place for a heaven-forsaken rock, but wherever I may be,

and whatever may befall me, I will aye have a warm
heart to St. Kilda."

Lost to sight in the bed of a burn and the rifts
of the rock, it was some little time before they
emerged above the beach of the anchorage. The
natives, who were evidently on the outlook, saw
them, but made no sign ; they were gathered round
a boat's crew who had landed.

" Why do they not hasten with the news ?" asked
Lady Grange, impatiently.

" They'll be grieved to lose you, madam. It will be
a sorrowful day for the poor bodies," answered Jessie,
but she, too, seemed surprised and anxious. With
palpitating hearts and uncertain steps, they made
their way towards the shore, and then such a wail
as had been sent up at Hesker rose from the little
assemblage.

" God bless them," said Lady Grange. " They
have been good to me in my adversity, and may He
forget me now and for ever, if I do not remember
them in prosperity."

If Jessie heard, she made no response. She saw
her father in the little crowd, and she misliked it
that he did not hasten to meet them. The lady

moved onward with a light step, and Jessie followed. The faces of the islanders were sullen and threatening, while the new comers seemed to draw apart and keep on their guard. As for the catechist, he stood aside, with arms folded and eyes on the ground. Then one of the strangers, with pistols in his belt, and a cutlass under his arm, stepped forward. Raising a hand to his bonnet, he accosted Lady Grange with respectful civility. Jessie flashed a searching glance of intelligence at him, which he avoided sheepishly. Yet he was a stalwart young fellow, with a frank, manly face, more like a stalker of the deer than a seaman. He looked a likely lad to steal a maiden's heart, or to take it by storm, for the matter of that, if it offered resistance. He glanced timidly at the St. Kilda beauty, but he addressed Lady Grange with a courtesy that was by no means awkward. Perhaps he might have been less abrupt; but Malcolm, with the feelings of a gentleman, had not the usages of society.

"Will it please your ladyship to make up your mails with what speed you may. The wind's shifting about through all the airts, and we would do well to weigh anchor with the evening's ebb."

"That will I do willingly. And yet," she added, after a moment's thought, "I would like to have longer time to bid farewell to my friends here. But, doubtless, you bring me letters?" and she held out her hand.

"I—have—no—letters, madam," he stammered out slowly; for though he avoided looking at Jessie, he felt her eyes were fixed on him.

"No letters! But you are bidden to take me to Edinburgh?"

He shuffled his feet on the sand, but was ominously silent.

Now Lady Grange understood it all. This time the shock was grievous. For once she had welcomed hope, and cherished it till it had taken up its abode with her. She shook and trembled; yet, as if she disdained to make her agony a spectacle for the curious onlookers, she controlled her emotion with a mighty effort. But the face which had been radiant and benignant a moment before, grew hard and set as it had been. The kindly light died out of her eyes, and they kindled with the sullen fire which Jessie knew so well, and which used at once to terrify and attract her. She

muttered, but in tones so low that they were heard
by none but the girl nestling up to her, "Deceived
and betrayed again. Abandoned by man to the
cruelty of my enemies, and forsaken by God, when
for once I was fool enough to trust in Him!"

Jessie clutched her arm, again forgetting respect
for rank and station.

"You dinna believe, my lady, that my father
or I have played you false? Surely, by now, you
have learned to trust me?"

For the time her ladyship had lost trust in
everything and everybody; but she could not resist
the pleading look and streaming eyes.

"No, my lassie; I do believe that you, at any
rate, have been true to me. But as for your God,
and all the psalms and texts you have been reading
to me——"

"Oh, my lady, dinna blaspheme. He has putten
you again into the fiery furnace, but be assured you
were never dearer to Him than you are now."

Lady Grange said nothing to that. She would
have answered the girl with a caress had they
been alone; she only put her aside with a gentle
touch. She turned to Malcolm.

" I suppose, sir, that you must obey the behests of those who have sent you, but if your orders permit it, I shall be glad to have the night to take leave of my dear friend, Miss McAlpine. Such sort of partings are painful at the best. I do not enquire whither you are taking me, but I know who have commissioned you ; and this I know, besides, that she and me will never meet again on this side the grave.''

Jessie looked at Malcolm, frowning and ruffling her plumes, like a dove who had turned to a falcon. Never would he have believed that those dove-like eyes could have sent forth such fiery and imperious flashes. He shuffled again, and his Highland pride was irritated beyond endurance, that he should make a figure so pitiable before the girl of his heart and that other woman—were she bad or good—whom Jessie had taken to her friendship.

" I had my orders, it is true ; but d—n me if I promised to obey. The lady must go with us, that is a clear case. If she did not ship with me she would find a rougher conveyance. I could be none the better, and she muckle the waur. But she shall stay the night with you, Jessie, that I swear, even if the cutter drag her anchor, and the rocks rive her up into firewood."

He felt more than repaid for any betrayal of his employers by the glance Jessie threw back as she led the lady away. The catechist followed the pair. He was full of misplaced condolences and lamentations in his unfortunate lack of tact. The dutiful daughter, for once, was almost ashamed of her excellent father. The passionate Lady Grange never gave such a proof of her affection for Jessie as when she tolerated the platitudes without breaking out.

At last the women were closeted together in the hut. They lit the little cruzie, where the wick floated in the fulmar oil, and the lady sank back on the miserable bed, while Jessie seated herself opposite on a decrepit stool. Alone at last, for Jessie had come to count for nobody, the captive gave way to a storm of sobs and moans, broken by hardly articulate speech. When it did take intelligible form, it sounded like execration or hideous blasphemy. Jessie sat silent, paralysed and horrified; it seemed to her that the powers of evil were there in personal presence, that the great tempter had got the better of her at last, in the prolonged and fluctuating war they had been waging for this storm-tossed soul. But like the wise girl she was, she bided her time. This storm was too violent to last; when it spent itself, her whispers might be heard in the calm.

Long she pled, when the time came, and the lady listened, or seemed to listen. But her heart was hardened, as it well might be. The old demon of revenge had seized her again, and he found his former habitation swept and garnished, thanks to the care of his servants, Lovat and Grange. The only coherent answer to entreaty and expostulation was—

"It was folly to think of changing my fate. I was doomed from the birth and the marriage-bed to reprobation. What else could you expect of the daughter of Dalry and the wife of Grange. I was born under a heavy curse to be the victim of a thousand wrongs, and the only saying in the Scriptures in which I believe is that the sins of the fathers are visited on the children. But Chiesley's vengeance has become a bye-word in the Scotland that has been ever dyed deep in blood and

crime, and I well believe I will yet-a-while be preserved to show that Rachel Erskine is her father's
child ! "

" And she is parting from us in the morning!"
exclaimed Jessie, wringing her hands in anguish
and impotence. She felt as if her hardly-won
convert was hanging over a bottomless abyss, from
which she was holding her back by the skirt of a
garment that was slipping through her fingers.
Her arguments and her simple eloquence had lost
all their effect.

" You preach patience," said Lady Grange,
" when hope is gone and resignation dead. That
I shall be spared for vengeance, I am still assured,
and now that God casts me off, I shall turn back
for help to Satan. When I have looked my last
upon you, I have broken with all that is good."

Jessie had been thinking and planning while the
lady was tossing and turning in her paroxyms.

" But you have not looked your last upon me.
You saved my life that day, and I will never let go
my grip on you. You see, my lady, Malcolm—"
she hesitated, and the lady almost smiled. " You
see, my lady, I have, maybe, something to say to

Malcolm, and I'll fleech with him to let me keep you company, when you sail."

"And you would have your way, if anybody could, but he dare not do it, even if he were willing. Nor would I have you risk your life on my wretched fortunes. And there's your father, besides——"

"For my father, as he said himself only yesterday, he is over boots or brogues in the business already. He is well assured he'll have to flit from St. Kilda, whether he will or no. As for Malcolm, though his will may be good, it's possible he may be compelled to deny me the passage. That's very true. If he landed me on the Long Island, beknown to your ill-wishers, it would be but keeping me in the Lewis till they sent me back again. Aye, I have thought of that, and it might be all ordered for the best."

"No doubt," said the lady, ironically.

"Aye, no doubt; but ye dinna take me. For if I dinna company your ladyship, I could carry your plaints to Edinburgh mysel'. I'll speak to your husband and plead your cause. I'll pray him to free you from your captivity, as you have heartily forgiven him, for you *had* forgiven him freely, as

R

you said but yesternight. Take patience yet, madam, and oh, dinna fling away your faith! If you but remain steadfast, all will end aright, one way or another."

"Aye, one way or another. But would you dare so much for me? I do not say your success would be richly rewarded; but think of the danger and the cost. It is folly even to dream of it, and the journey would be bootless, forbye. Grange would never see you, or he would have you put out of sight and hearing, like myself. You would be risking liberty for a fruitless errand."

"I know otherwise, madam, and my mind is fixed. Keep up your heart, happen what may, and always look out for the glimmer of the bow in the clouds."

Jessie saw duly to the packing of the trunks; it was soon despatched, and with little trouble. Then, with the break of dawn, she sought an interview with Malcolm. He was relieved and gratified by that act of grace, the rather that his lady-love came with gentle words and winning smiles. Perhaps night watching and deadly anxiety had drawn dark circles round the tearful eyes, but he had never seen her more bewitching. He must have been more or less than a man, and a Highland lover, had he not been willing to do her reasonable bidding. But as to shipping the beauty for a passenger, he was obdurate.

"It's clean out o' the question, my darling, and fruitless to the back of that. You would be parted from her as soon as you set feet on the shore."

Jessie had feared as much, and like the sensible girl she was, she yielded, or seemed to yield. But her retreat only marked an approach from another direction.

"And so you will do nothing for me?" she pouted, with a saucy glance, for simple as she was, she could use the weapons of her sex.

"Ask anything in reason, and ye will see what I would do for you."

"Well," she said, laying a caressing hand on his shoulder, "tell me, anyhow, whither they are taking her."

"I know as little as yourself or the babe unborn."

"You can find out."

"I know not that. My duty is done when I have landed the lady."

"A fine duty, to harm a helpless woman! I could never have thought it of you."

"If the woman be harmless, she is the more misjudged; and how could I tell that you cared, one way or another?"

"Well, you can tell now it's more than caring, Malcolm. If that lady come to any mischief through your means, I will never touch your hand again. I'm asking nothing you cannot do, and, see, the folk are beginning to stir. Give me your solemn promise that you will never lose sight of her; maybe that will content me—in the meantime."

Malcolm stole an arm round the waist of his lady-love, and she did not seem to observe it. He scratched his brow meditatively with his other hand, and then he burst out—

"They told me to hold my peace, and seek to know nothing of secrets that might knot a tow round my neck. But I gave them neither pledge nor promise, and I'd chance the woodie any day for the sake of winning you. If so much will satisfy ye, I swear that I will follow the woman and her keepers over ferry and hill, through heather and peat moss. I'll sleep out in my plaid, and live on bannocks and burn water, and they'll be clever chiels if, with all their wiles, they can hide their track from the eyes of the best stalker in Applecross."

"I'll trust you," was the answer, and Malcolm took pay for his chivalry on the spot by folding his arms round the island beauty and passionately kissing her lips.

She disengaged herself, blushing, but not offended. In gratitude and common Christian charity she was bound to discharge her debts of honour. Waiving him off further familiarity, she made him happy, nevertheless, by saying she was going to ask another favour which would not interfere with his duty. "A favour I would ask of no other living creature but my father." Then she told him of her fixed determination to travel to Edinburgh. Naturally, he exclaimed and protested. To the Highlander, who had himself never been farther south than Oban, such a journey for an unprotected female seemed tremendous, if not impracticable.

Nor could anything Jessie urged move him from that position, till at last she said—

"And you have never heard yet the favour I was to ask. My father's bit stipend is a term behindhand, and for myself, I have not a penny Scots. I was meaning to beg you for a gold piece or two to put in my purse for the way, and if you still set your face against my travelling, I'll think that you grudge me."

That argument, joined to Jessie's evident determination, proved decisive. Malcolm, like a wise man, yielded in the meantime to a will he could not bend, and like a generous man, produced a leathern bag from his breast pocket. Carefully undoing the string which tied it, he poured out a handful of silver pieces, with a sprinkling of gold. Though a free-handed fellow, and a lover to boot, he knew how hardly the money had been come by; and perhaps he liked his mistress none the worse for the moderation which contented itself with two or three guineas, and resolutely refused anything more.

On second thoughts, though infinitely grateful and deeply touched, moreover, Jessie was less satisfied with the situation. Her "friend" had done as much as she had hoped, and far, far more than she had any right to expect. With the frugal upbringing which had taught her the value of pence, she was well fitted to appreciate his lavish liberality. She knew how hardly those gold pieces had been won, how penuriously they must have been saved, and her heart whispered to her of the purpose with which he had been treasuring them. He had done as much as a man might to help her, but how was she to be passed over to the mainland. It would be full three months at the least, before the annual ship from Stornoway was due. So she was the less surprised that Lady Grange was rather depressed than elated. "You had better give up all idea of your wild scheme," said the lady, "it may be three months, or it may be six, before you have a chance of sailing, and who can tell what may happen in that time? As your father would say, it has all been wisely ordered, for you would only have endangered yourself, without doing good to me. My doom is fixed," and she sank down upon her corded boxes.

Jessie could only comfort her with vague

generalities, and having no assured conviction herself, gave up the task in despair. She stepped out to have a talk with her father—not that she expected assistance from him. Instinctively she breathed a prayer to heaven, but to tell the truth, it was sadly lacking in faith. Then she saw Malcolm, impatiently pacing the beach; he had clearly been keeping a watch on the door of the cabin.' He hastened towards her as soon as she appeared. That was natural enough, but he plunged forthwith into business, as a man who misdoubts his own resolution.

"I've been thinking over your matter."

"Oh, surely, Malcolm, you're not meaning to draw back."

"You never heard I was in the way of breaking my promises," said Malcolm, with dignity; "least of all, when my word was passed to you. What I was thinking was this, that I've promised enough to make mortal enemies of men in high places."

"And it was I who made ye. Well, well, it would be wicked of me to hold you to your words."

"To tell the clean truth, Jessie, ye did beguile me, as you might beguile me again. Ye can twist me round your little finger, and we are bound together for better or worse. And, God, my lass, that fact alone is enough to give a man courage if he wanted it. As I was saying, what I was thinking was this: I might as well be hanged for a drift of cattle as for a single sheep, and I'll give ye a cast over to the Lewis, and put ye in a safe way of getting to the South. There'll be spies and enemies watching our landing, no doubt, but I can smuggle ye on board of the brig of a friend that is taking in cargo for Oban, and the master'll pass ye on, and put ye in a way of getting to Glasgow."

"But what is to happen to you?"

"I'll know nothing, except that I kindly gave you a lift across, and there'll need know nothing till you're ayont the Moil" (the Mull of Cantyre), "and I'm lying out on the braes of Lochalsh or Lochaber. And may God forgive me for all the lees I will have to tell," he added, *sotto voce*, "for Jessie never would."

CHAPTER XVI.

THE LAST PARTING OF THE WAYS.

ONE unexpected sensation is apt to lead on to another, like a stone making " ducks and drakes " on the surface of a still pool. Old Elspeth Mc-Alpine had been astounded by the arrival of the missive in the ball of wool. She was at least as much astonished when one fine morning a young woman walked in upon her, and announced herself as her niece from St. Kilda. Had Elspeth been more suspicious than she was, she could never have mistaken her visitor, with the pleasant face and the frank smile, for an impostor. She took her to her arms at once, and did her best to warm and make her comfortable, with many apologies for poor hospitality. Highland-like, she asked no questions till her guest had "shifted herself," and been warmed and fed; but then there was matter enough for amazement and alarm. Elspeth heard to her sorrow and indignation how entirely her interposition had failed; but the failure gave her even an exaggerated idea of the power for evil of Lovat and Grange. "If the Lord Advocate and the Lord Justice, not to speak of that feckless body Monypenny, can do nothing, what can you do, my lass? Get to speech o' my Lord Grange! Aye, doubtless that might be contrived, though it would be ill to do; but what after that? If he did not even spare the wife of his bosom, for all her birth and blood, and kinsfolk; if he could draw the straws over the eyes of the Advocate, when he should have been sent to the Tolbooth, and on to the Plantations, what chance will there be for you, if you threaten them with stirring the stour? It would cost Lovat nothing—and he's in the town the now, they tell me—to have ye caught up by twa-three o' his gillies, and taken down in the gloaming to Leith or the Queensferry. There are aye ships in the Firth for America, or maybe for France; and there might be waur than death or bonds for a bonnie lassie like yoursel'."

Though Jessie had realized good part of that, she shivered involuntarily; but nothing her grand-aunt could urge would shake her.

"I came hither on an errand of mercy, having counted the cost ; I maun trust to God to take care o' the rest. As He hath led me hitherto, He will guide me still."

"It's very true," responded the old lady dubiously. "Nathless, it's just as weel no to tempt the Almighty too far."

Nevertheless, next morning, Grange's old servant, Peter, somewhat aged, but more familiarly respectful than ever—for he was deeper in his master's secrets than my lord would have desired, announced that there was "one wanting to speak to him."

Grange had sat late at supper, and drank deeply.

"Bid him be off, then, you old gomeril. You should know better than to come troubling me at this time of day."

"It's no a him, but a her," said Peter, drily. "And a weel-faured lassie to boot, weel putten on, and with a blink in her eyes like the sun on the sea-foam."

Grange's face relaxed. The old gallant had always a soft heart for the fair sex.

"Why, you grow poetical on us, Peter, my man ; but show the lassie ben. But, stay—bide a bit," and he stepped aside into his sleeping chamber to adjust his periwig and change slippers for buckled shoes.

He received his visitor with graceful condescension, mingling the formal dignity of the old Scottish seigneur with the ease of the man of the world who would gladly renew his youth. The face predisposed him in favour of the petitioner, and the seriousness of the expression gave it additional piquancy; for that the girl came as a petitioner he did not for a moment doubt.

So she did come; but it need hardly be said that the nature of the petition staggered him. All idea of frivolity or senile flirtation was gone. The sweet face was a Medusa's head that might have frozen him to stone; but he rallied when he felt the crisis needed all his faculties. Weakly, or to have time to think, he tried to carry matters with a high hand; but he knew that it was not so he could get rid of this girl. The journey she had undertaken for a persecuted stranger was proof sufficient of her earnestness and determination. Lovat, doubtless, would have cut such an interview short, and as the less dangerous way out of a dangerous dilemma, would have taken measures for the sure custody of the intruder. The ex-Lord Justice was more scrupulous, and had an innate regard for the law he used to administer. Besides, he was cast in very different mould. He had a conscience, as we know, which might nod or doze, but never actually slept. He could not choose but lend a feverish ear to the girl's impassioned language. With simple eloquence she painted the mental struggles she had witnessed; the sore battle with long-cherished vengeance which was ending in the calm of Christian forgiveness, and in an act of remorseful oblivion for all the wrongs she had endured.

"The battle was well nigh won, my lord, and I was rejoicing in her salvation, when the message came that has torn her from the friends she had made, and doomed her again to the darkness of despair. Had the dove of peace come over the seas with the olive branch, her wrongs would have been forgiven, and you were safe from the consequences of conduct which it is not for the like of me to judge. Now, I am in doubt. But, oh, my lord, bethink you, when yet there is time. If she be spared, I make bold to be her warrant that she will do you no mischief; but if she dies in your hands, she will be gone to plead her case at the Judgment-seat. How you may answer her, maun rest with yourself."

Had she been the most astute advocate at the Scottish Bar, briefed by the shrewdest Writer to the Signet, she could not have appealed more forcibly to Grange's peculiar temperament. With his habitual vacillation, he was a man much given to speculate on what might have been, had he acted differently. He had suffered Lovat to take this last piece of business absolutely out of his hands, though with many searchings of heart; and now Lovat's fine-drawn and relentless sagacity had brought them both unnecessarily to shipwreck. But a consideration weighing with him infinitely more, was that he might have conjured the spectres of terror and remorse which ever since the fatal kidnapping had made his life unceasing misery.

It would have been well for him had he listened to the last earnest whispers of his better self, taken a manly resolution at the moment, and decided for himself. But the Judge's caution, and the fear of irritating the Highland Mephistopheles were too strong for him. "I'll sleep upon it," he said to himself, "and see in the morning what had best be done." To Jessie he addressed abundant assurances, but though she knew he was not insincere at the time, somehow the girl misdoubted. Born and brought up as she had been at the back of the world, her instincts seemed to warn her that the old statesman was weak—a reed that would be shaken by the shifting of the wind. But she had got her dismissal, and natural politeness forbade her to linger. She had had her interview, she had fulfilled her mission, yet with a woman's peace and a human soul at stake, she was loth to leave the work unfinished. She seized Lord Grange's hand and touched it respectfully with her lips. Her clear eyes looked up into those others which were bleared and somewhat shifty: "As you do by her, sir, remember, so God will deal by you;" then, without waiting for an answer, she curtsied and withdrew.

Grange, although his resolutions were good, wished she had spared him that last look, which was likely to live in his memory. He lived in

terror of the phantoms that haunted him, nor did
he desire to add to their number. So he dined
and drank, and slumbered, and started, and woke,
and supped and drank again,—meditating all the
time around the subject from which he shrank,
but which nevertheles preoccupied his wandering
thoughts and dazed faculties.

When Peter called him in the morning, seasoned
cask as he was, his head was aching and his palate
parched.

"Will ye have your small beer or a hair of the
dog that has bitten you?" demanded Peter, respectfully. His lordship elected for the beer, and then
tried the brandy. As his brain cleared a little, he
felt all the worse. He would send for Lovat. He
would not send for Lovat. He would act for himself; he dared not act for himself, after all that
a was come and gone. He had slipped his neck in
tippet of tow, and if he were false to old comrade-
ship, the tow would be tightened. So he might
have gone on tossing and hesitating, but the matter
was settled for him.

A resounding knock at the door of the flat was
followed by Peter's reappearance.

"It's him of Lovat, my lord. Will I show him into your bed-chamber here, or will ye wait upon him in the dining parlour? He bid me say his business is pressing, and he maun see ye forthwith."

"So you have had the bonny lass from St. Kilda with you, you hardened scant o' grace?" was Lovat's greeting, and it took Grange aback. He was shaken and full of aches and tremors, and it struck him for the hundredth time that his omniscient friend must be the very fiend in human form.

"You are surprised I should know about it," proceeded his lordship, genially; "but it's my business, as you should have discovered by this time, to take care of you and myself, and my information is good, as you have reason to know. Well, these matters are all being managed for the best, for I was thinking we could afford now to come to terms with God and the lady. Maybe we drove things with her a bit farther than was needful, but it's aye time to repent, if we were in the wrong, and make reparation."

Grange was astounded. To find Lovat ready to give effect to his desires, and to assist him in easing his burdened conscience, was indeed a special interposition of Providence, an unexpected answer to the prayers he had been alternating with curses.

"I thought that your last notion was to take her away from St. Kilda—against my judgment—and put her in yet safer keeping, somewhere out of sight on the mainland."

"It was so; but since then I've been learning something more of her mind. I'm thinking that solitude has restored her to her senses, and that we might have her back in the South on satisfactory guarantees. It's aye time to be merciful, with due regard to yourself."

Grange was inexpressibly relieved. His faith in Lovat's astuteness was unlimited. If the politic Simon talked of safety in the circumstances, his conscience would be eased without risking the penalties of his offences in a public prosecution or social ostracism.

"No doubt the St. Kilda lass," added Lovat, pleasantly, "has well deserved the lady's confidence. My faith! and she well may, for few folks would have perilled as much. It's evident that we

can do no better than make her our messenger and
send her back hotfoot and at once. Doubtless the
girl's short of siller, and we must contrive to spare
her a few broad pieces for her travelling. A trusty
follower of mine will see her safe to Greenock, and
give my instructions to the shipman who carries
her North to find her a guide to your lady's new
quarters in Lochaber. Is she coming here again?
Not that you know of, you say. Well, then, make
haste with your breakfast and draw on your boots,
and we'll go and have speech with her in her
grandmother's—grandaunt's—garret."

Still with throbbing head and tangled thoughts,
Grange yielded to the dictation of the master-spirit.
He merely remarked, "It may be you'll find her
harder of belief than you think for;" to which
the only answer was a smile.

Elspeth and Jessie were seated over the fire,
talking the same talk for the hundredth time.
Would Grange see her again? Would he send for
her, or send to her? When should she know if her
appeal had been successful? There were footsteps
on the stair and a rapping at the door. The worthy
old woman was not yet broken to such surprises,

and when she opened, she was struck dumb. There was the worshipful Lord Grange, whom she knew by sight, like all his townsfolk, in a rich though sober suit, befitting his dignity, and behind him a commanding figure in dark tartan, with the haughty yet condescending bearing that became a chieftain of birth! Seldom had such visitors climbed to the tenth story of the tenement in the Laigh closes. Grange introduced himself and friend, with patrician courtesy, and the old Highland dame, who trembled before the brother of the Earl of Mar and a Lord of Justiciary, almost sank to the floor at the name of Lovat. No man of the day, in all Scotland, was more universally feared or more generally mistrusted. But it was that affable gentleman who took the word and hastened to reassure her. He softened his somewhat grating accents into a kindly Highland lisp, and for the benignant smiles that beamed on his face he might have just descended from the seventh heaven like St. Paul. When Elspeth dusted a chair, mumbling something about her garret being no place for the like of them, he cut her short with winning familiarity.

"We both come from the Highlands, and my

heart always warms to the Highland folk. You and I must have a crack about the North and old times, but meantime, my good lord has brought me here to make your niece's acquaintance."

He bowed to Jessie with the reverence he might have paid to a Court beauty. It might have passed for mockery, but a wary diplomatist might have been deceived by the frank cordiality of his manner, and as he passed his hand, with a soft paternal touch, over Jessie's curls, she began to think the good chieftain had been sorely calumniated. He read the girl at a glance, and was far too adroit to flatter her too far. But he spoke with deep feeling of his appreciation of the courage and devotion she had exhibited.

" You judge us hardly, no doubt, and such is my admiration of your unselfishness, that I would wish to set myself right with you. You've only heard the lady's side of the case, and you may believe the word of a Highland gentleman, Miss Jessie, that there's something to be said on the other. I might mind you of the text, ' Judge not, that ye be not judged.' Yet I'll grant you that the lady may have had hard measure: when women have a looser tongue than yours', those they threaten cannot always stand on trivialities. I'll grant you again, that we may have been sometimes mistaken. But now the time is come for which my Lord Grange and I have always been longing and praying, and we are blythe to take your word that your friend, or rather your client, as they say in the Courts, is willing to forget and forgive. I know well I can do you no greater pleasure than to bid the fair blue rock dove from St. Kilda fly back to the North. We set our necks in peril if the Lady Grange break her pledges, and put false tales and poisoned weapons in the hands of our bloodthirsty enemies; but we are both of us old and failing, and it signifies but little. The end of my pilgrimage is very near now, and fain would I die at peace with all men."

Had Jessie been looking his lordship in the small twinkling eyes, her shrewd sense might have taken alarm. As she had kept her own bashfully on the floor, she began to think the calumniated Lovat little short of a saint. None the less, that he might be a penitent sinner. The upshot was that she humbly acquiesced in all his arrangements, and was only anxious to hasten back with the good news.

Knowing the state of Lady Grange's moral and bodily health, the days and even the hours were invaluable. Moreover, she remembered the dangers to which Malcolm might be exposed, when he was scouting in her service, among broken men who were reckless and desperate. As she was almost penniless, she scarcely scrupled at accepting the gold which Lovat generously bestowed. In those days no inferior would have dreamed of refusing the careless bounty of a grand seigneur. And that evening Jessie thanked heaven on her knees for the special miracles that had been wrought in her favour, and for the thoughtful arrangements which facilitated her return.

As for Grange, though he ought to have known his friend better than the unsophisticated Miss MacAlpine, he was in a fool's paradise. His nerves were steadied and his spirits rose. If Lovat were satisfied, all must be right. His lady would come back, ready to let byegones be byegones, and they would live apart in amicable separation. He was willing to make her a respectable allowance, and it was paying cheaply for the lifting of the weight from his conscience. "At last, I will be

once more my own man again," he said to himself.
And so, having recovered from his previous night's
debauch, he readily adjourned with Lovat to
" Fortune's." In the fear of having his new-found
tranquility disturbed, he said nothing directly on
the subject that preoccupied both.   But the worthy
boon-companions quoted Scripture generally as to
the duty of forgiveness, and the blessings on the
merciful; they jested in unfatherly fashion with
the merry serving wenches ; the pious talk became
loose and licentious; and with cracked voices they
intoned odd staves of glees which would have
shocked the not over-scrupulous Edinburgh Pres-
bytery.   Perhaps the evening might not have passed
off so agreeably had Grange been collected enough
to catch the sardonic smile with which his friend
sometimes regarded him.

CHAPTER XVII.

Ἀνάγκη.

ON each day of Jessie's journey to the North she had reason to be grateful for Lord Lovat's forethought. The thoughtful old nobleman had made every arrangement for her comfort. She travelled to Oban under the wing of a kindly Highland dame who chanced to be going thither, and who was full of praises of the free-handed chief of her clan. The good lady's sincerity was not to be mistaken, for she had substantial proof of the chieftain's bounty. "And all he gives he gives freely," she said, "for he has nothing to get by helping the like o' me." One unfortunate hitch there was, for the brig in which Jessie was to have taken passage had sailed with the tide the very afternoon they arrived. There was some unlucky misunderstanding, but it did not greatly signify, for a swifter sloop was to set forth in a day or two. Even when matters of life and death were concerned, such delays were accepted as inevitable by the wayfarers who committed themselves to the fogs and currents of the Western seas. Indeed, the master of the brig had been Jessie's *avant-courrier*, for when she landed at the Gairloch after a stormy voyage, seasick and sorely shaken, she was helped ashore by a decent-looking elderly Celt, who told her he had orders to guide her to her destination. A night's rest in the little change-house restored her, and next morning she was up with the lark, to find a shaggy pony in waiting at the door, to carry herself and her slender baggage. Side-saddle there was none, but Jessie could accommodate herself on the pad, with a plaid gathered round her knees to serve for a riding-skirt.

Preoccupied and eager to arrive as she was, she nevertheless enjoyed the rough ride. The smell of the peat, the bloom of the fragrant heather, the shrill cry of the muirfowl flitting across the track, the whistle of the shy curlew, and the scream of the eagle, were all delightfully homelike after the home-sickness of the sojourn in Edinburgh smoke. Yet she would have been happier could she have taken more kindly to her conductor. As to his conduct, there was nothing to complain of. He was by her side at the bad bits in the mosses; he laid hold of her bridle in fording the rushing streams; when the fog fell thick and changed to a cold drizzle, he drew her wrappings carefully around her. But he was silent and sombre; black-avised with heavy beetling brows: like the ghost she fancied him, when striding before her, phantom-like, through the mist, he never spoke except when spoken to, and then his answers were short. When the sun broke out, and all nature seemed rejoicing in the beams, his face alone caught no light from the sunshine. He looked as if he were oppressed by some weighty anxiety, but Jessie reproached herself. Lord Lovat knew and trusted him, and surely that was enough. Gravity was a common characteristic of the High-landers, bred and brought up in the sad sterility of their lonely glens. If he were abrupt and reserved when she sought to question him, no one could be more assiduously attentive, and he was clearly a man under authority.

As they advanced the country became wilder and wilder; the hamlets and shealings were very

few and far between. Though the guide appeared
tolerably familiar with the districts, more than
once they wandered aside from the track, to be
brought up by the burn they had followed plunging over a precipice, or by some quaking bog in the
velvet-covered peat-flow, when the pony, snorting
in apprehension, sturdily refused to budge. Nor
could they call local knowledge to their aid, when
for leagues and dreary leagues they never set eyes
on living soul. The wild-eyed black cattle ranging
these wastes at will would crowd up to stare, then
turn to take flight, kicking up their heels. The
lordly stag would rise from his lair in the heather,
stare in excited amazement like the cattle,
and trot quietly away, turning to gaze over his
haunches. He was so seldom disquieted that he
was ignorant of fear. Once, when night surprised
them, they had to lie out on the hillside. Jessie's
guide, an old hill-wanderer, had stopped in time
to search her out a cavity or cave in a sheltered
hollow, where he strewed her a soft bed of heather
shoots, sleeping out himself in the open in his
plaid. They had a frugal supper of bannocks and
ewe-milk cheese from his game-pouch, with water

from the burn dashed with the whisky. Never did
Jessie commend herself more earnestly to the care
of Providence than when she lay down on the
couch of heather. Weary as she was, sleep soon
overtook her, but the rest was fitful and broken.
In the long intervals of troubled waking, she
listened to the hoarse snoring of her guardian,
and the cropping of the hobbled shelty, to the
wail of the wild-cats from a neighbouring cairn,
and to the night-bark of the marauding fox on the
prowl. When she stretched herself and looked
out at the first faint breaking of the rosy dawn,
the fire of bog oak had burned down to grey ashes,
and a pair of venerable ravens were hopping round
the sleeping Highlander, as if they had scented a
prey and claimed a corpse. When she shook an
arm at them, with sullen and resentful croak they
merely fluttered to a stone a few yards away, as
if the feast they counted on were only deferred.
The healthy Highland-bred girl had never felt so
strangely depressed; she saw in the sinister
familiarity of these birds of evil omen a warning
that her errand had come to nought. The sense
of utter desolation was brought home to her.

Anything might happen in these lawless wastes, and the great gentlemen of the law in the remote metropolis were as powerless to avenge as to prevent. The lady had passed that way before, not under the fatherly protection of Lovat, but in the charge of men who set the law at defiance, and might deem it good service to get rid of her. She thought very tenderly of Malcolm, who doubtless was watching on those hills; it might be within a mile or two, or it might be many a league away. She would give anything to hear his honest voice, and to feel his stalwart arm around her. But he was better employed, and that was her comfort.

They never had occasion to bivouac on the hillside again, though their best night quarters gave little more than a leaky shelter from the wet, and bannocks of the coarsest barley with goat's milk. The rough living and the hard lying told alike on the girl's health and spirits, and the tension on her nerves was becoming well-nigh insupportable, when her taciturn companion relieved her with the intelligence that before nightfall they would reach their destination. It was relief in one sense, but the suspense and excitement seemed to touch her brain. Involuntarily her hands went up to her throbbing forehead, and for once she feared seriously for her reason. She asked herself if she could hold out till satisfied somehow. Would she arrive in time or too late? Had the lady, with her extraordinary courage and strength of will, borne up against disappointment and bodily suffering, or had she finally given herself over to vindictive despair, and renounced her Saviour for Satan?

Indeed, the scene she looked down upon from the summit of a low pass seemed a fitting spot for the culmination of a dismal tragedy. The pass plunged through a precipitous gorge into the depths of a valley that had the gloom of Glencoe without its sublimity. The barren hills closed in upon the course of the burn that wound its way through peat-flow and quaking morass; and on a slightly elevated plateau stood a solitary shealing, which could scarcely be distinguished from the rugged surroundings. It was built of turf, thatched with heather or rushes. What an abode for a well-nurtured lady! After her sight of Edinburgh, and the almost luxurious chamber of Lord Grange, Jessie could only think, without analysing her thoughts, of the strange vicissitudes of this mortal existence and the vanity of all earthly things.

She was lifted off her pony at the door of the hut; two or three stalwart Highlanders were lounging about, who roused themselves to give greetings to her morose conductor; and an aged crone was standing in the low doorway, who did not greet the newcomer at all, but grumblingly stood aside to give her room to pass. Jessie stepped out of light into darkness, to plunge her foot in a puddle. A she-goat followed by her kid, bounded by under her arm, and there were the cackle and flutter of scared poultry. The only light came from the low door and from the straw-bound "lum" or chimney, through which the peat smoke escaped. She was familiar with the wretched dwellings of St. Kilda, but had seen nothing more miserable than this. As her waiting eyes became accustomed to the twilight, she could distinguish a low couch or truckle bed in a corner. She trod forward across the muddy floor and stooped over it. She saw a form huddled under plaids and

T

blankets, but though she could distinguish nothing of the features, she made sure it was her friend. For all distinctions of rank were forgotten now ; or rather, the high-born lady and the catechist's daughter had changed their places. Jessie sank sobbing on the bed, and clasped the figure in her arms. Lady Grange woke up and thrust her away with a scream, like the trapped wild creature who sees an enemy everywhere. Then as she felt the throbbing of the bosom and heard the broken sobs, she burst out in a joyful cry.

"And so you have come back to me, and in time, Jessie. I thought that I was doomed to die alone."

"Never speak of dying yet, my lady. I trust you may live yet through many a happy day. I bring you good tidings of great joy, if I dare say so."

"Be they what they may, they are come too late. My suffering will soon be over, and the days of mourning in this world are overpast. As for the next——"

"Keep a good heart, madam, and all will be well with you yet, here and hereafter. Now you know that you are your own woman once more,

free to come and go as the winds, you will soon be
on your feet again. I ken your courage, and it
would take muckle to kill you."

Jessie strove to speak cheerfully, but she was
gravely alarmed. Now that her eyes were getting
accustomed to the darkness, she could see a sad
change in the invalid. The cheeks were sunken,
the nostrils were pinched, the lips were drawn, and
the complexion was livid. Now that the first
flutter of excitement had died down, the sick
woman had fallen back and was breathing heavily.
Jessie looked about for some medicine or restorative, but saw none. She turned to the old crone
who was standing beside her, but the hag seemed
to look on with profound indifference, and only
moaned and muttered something unintelligible.
She rushed out to seek assistance from her guide,
who, feeling that his duty was done, was silently
lighting a pipe among his companions, who pressed
him with questions. She asked for his whisky
bottle, and he stolidly handed it to her, without
sign of interest or look of surprise. She had
scarcely felt so much alone in the darkness and
the heart of the solitudes. Helpless she was,

unless she helped herself. She poured some of the spirit into a quaich; added water from an earthernware pot, lifted the lady on one arm, and held the cup to her lips. The medicine was sipped and then swallowed down greedily, and for the time the change was marvellous. Some light came back to the failing eye, and the lady spoke with something of the old energy.

"That's good: my old foe has turned friend at last. And what of the other enemies? You bring news, and I would fain hear them, but my time is short. I am a dying woman, and Lovat has done his worst."

"God forbid, my lady! The travel and the grief have been ower much for you, and little wonder. But listen to my news, and you'll soon be yourself again."

"I tell you that it's too late, and all is well nigh over. That woman there has poisoned me, and I don't blame *her*. She was bound to do her master's bidding."

Jessie hoped the invalid was wandering in her mind; the hardship, solitude, and fever had deranged her brain. But the belief was shaken

when Lady Grange told lucidly and intelligibly
how she had reached the hovel one night, weary,
but well in health ; how she had woke with a keen
appetite, and after breaking her fast, had been
seized with violent retchings and had sweated pro-
fusely. " I thought at the time that the milk had
a strange flavour, and now I know there was death
in the drink. I have never refused what they
offered me since, for I was done, and that one drink
was sufficient."

Jessie could not resist the horrible conviction
that the lady was speaking the simple truth. Of
a sudden, her eyes seemed to be opened as she
looked back on the immediate past. This would
explain Lovat's paternal kindness and generosity, so
absolutely inconsistent with his general character.
Was it likely that the Ethiopian would change his
skin for her sake at a moment's notice ? Grief-
stricken as she was, she felt natural irritation
when she remembered how she had been tricked
and befooled. Lovat she gave up as a villainous
reprobate ; but vividly, as the recent interviews
presented themselves to her, she was still inclined
to believe in Grange. It was impossible to mis-

doubt his sincerity. He too, old man of the world as he was, had been fooled like herself by the arch-hypocrite who could clothe himself in the garments of an angel of light. And so she could thank God that at the worst her errand had been far from bootless, for if the lady's hours were indeed numbered, she could yet reconcile the husband and the wife.

Her surprise was even greater than her joy when she found the task more easy than she could have hoped. The death-stricken woman seemed to welcome the idea that the lover of her prime had at last relented.

"I loved him well once," she said, "and surely he once loved me. Old memories are not to be lightly forgotten. If he has wrought me muckle wrong—he had wrong and no little provocation. I can see it now—and I would be fain for the sake of the old times to die at peace with him. You will write and tell him that, or you might see him again yourself; and now, before I am gone, I want you to make me a promise."

"If it be anything lawful," said Jessie, hesitatingly, for she was too cautious to pledge herself blindfold, and she had reason to mistrust the lady's moods.

"My breath is failing—I cannot reason. It's nothing that can do harm, but only good. Promise! promise ! "

"I do promise," said Jessie, slowly, anxious to calm the excitement.

"Then when you bear or write my message to Grange, when you carry him my parting blessing and my pardon, bid him have a care of you and your Malcolm when once you are wedded. Tell him you gave your promise in the dark here to his dying wife, and that she bound it on your conscience to pray him to fulfil my bequest. Tell him his dealing with you must be the seal of his penitence. Now trouble me no more, for I would gladly rest awhile."

Lady Grange was right in declaring that her hours were numbered. She lingered for a day or two, rallying at intervals, and night and day Jessie watched by her pillow. Her mood had softened, as it had been when they parted in hope at St. Kilda, and more than once she feebly expressed her pleasure that all vindictive feeling had passed away, and that she was dying in peace and goodwill with her husband.

Encouraged by her unwonted gentleness, Jessie ventured on a subject from which she had shrank. She feared to ask too much of frail humanity, and yet there was an imperative duty laid upon her, which she felt bound to discharge. So one evening she whispered solemnly—

"Remember Him who said 'Vengeance is Mine,' and to whom you are looking yourself for mercy and forgiveness. Can you say from the heart that you forgive all your enemies?"

"I have forgiven," said the lady, petulantly. "You have my message to my husband, and what more would you want?"

"And Lord Lovat?"

"What would you trouble me for?" exclaimed the lady, with a fierce flash of the old passion. "I was at peace, and you would strew my pillow with thorns. Think you that I have not been thinking of that, ever and anon, but I aye strove and I prayed to put the thought away from me. The Lord knows that our frame is dust, and He would never require impossibilities."

"Forgive that you may be forgiven."

"There you are again. I cannot and I will not.

Would you have me go before my Judge with a lie
on my lips? When I plead my cause before the
Judgment seat, it's Lovat and not me that will
have cause to tremble. I bear no malice to the
miserable old woman here that obeyed his behests,
but the curse I passed on that devil her master at
Polmaise must cling to him, and as God may help
me in my hour of extremity, I would not recall it if
I could. Would you have me die a hypocrite like
him?"

It was a question of casuistry which the girl dared
not decide, nor could she shake her penitent's fixed
resolution. Lady Grange breathed out her spirit,
seemingly in the peace she desired, but she died in
unquenched enmity to Lovat.

*   *   *   *

As for Jessie, she experienced the natural
reaction. Her high-pitched hopes had all been
blighted; instead of being the messenger of joy,
she had come north to a mournfully dubious
death-bed. She sorrowed over the woman she
had learned to love, and to whom her life had
latterly been so devoted that for the moment she
could look no farther. Everything was wrapped

in impenetrable gloom. She doubted and almost
despaired of her penitent's destiny. Lady Grange
had changed so greatly at the last that she could
scarcely think the good work would be left unfinished. But if she had forgiven much, and died
conscientiously honest, she had let the eternal twilight settle down upon her deadly wrath. Jessie's
own sound nerves were fearfully overstrung
by travel, night-watching, semi-starvation, and
incessant worry. It was already dull and sullen
without, with the leaden and lowering skies and
the approaching sunset. Within, the hovel was
more dimly lighted by the glimmer of the rush-
lights and the flicker of the fire. The old mistress
of the place, apparently indifferent to the death,
was rocking herself on a " creepie " over the
smouldering peat, and croning a ditty which she
seemed to mean for a song of jubilation. The
whole situation was horrible; the stifling and
pungent atmosphere was morally and physically
intolerable. Jessie could not remain shut up with
the murderess and the corpse. She literally could
take no thought for the morrow; but, meantime,
she must have a breath of the caller air on any

terms. She threw a plaid around her shoulders
and went out. She passed the Highlanders,
huddled—as usual towards evening—around their
watch-fire; as careless of the death as the old
woman, they were smoking, talking, and laughing.
The bottles lying near accounted for their good
spirits, and they never stirred themselves to
challenge her. If they had charge to keep a
guard upon her, whither could she fly? The
mountains and the moss pits were effectual prison
walls. So she knew not, and scarcely cared what
her fate might be. She must wait to see the lady
laid in the grave, and then it would be time enough
to pray for direction. She strolled on amid the
darkening shadows of rock and rifted hollow.
Already the birds of the wastes were seeking
their roosting places, and as yet none of the night
hunters or prowlers were abroad. No sounds were
to be heard, save the soft soughing of a warm west
wind, the murmur of the burn at the bottom of the
glen, and the distant rush of a cataract.

Then she started to a shrill but low whistle.
She was not altogether incredulous in that darkening hour of the popular legends of the good people,

and the brownies and other mysterious beings which were still believed to haunt the morasses and the moorlands. Had she been given to swooning, she might have swooned on the spot; as it was, she merely shuddered and stood to listen. Then there came a delicious sense of relief and security, as she heard the well-known voice which heralded the well-known figure. If Malcolm had ever had cause to complain of her coyness, now he might be satisfied. She threw herself into his arms and clung to him convulsively. The strong arms were around her, and for the first time for many days she felt safe. After caressing her with a fervour she neither resisted nor resented, her lover found words at last.

"Aye, it's myself and no other. Did you think I would be far from you at a time like this?" But now we are thegither again, and how is it with the lady?"

Then Jessie poured everything into his ears. She told him of the suspicions, or rather certainty, of foul practices.

"I misdoubted as much," said Malcolm, gloomily. "I could do nothing forbye follow as you bid me,

for she was well watched. And when I saw where
they had taken her I feared the worst. That deevil
of a Lovat, when he is hard driven, is capable of
any darksome deed, and as for Auld Elspeth, the
crookback, with whom you are housed to your
sorrow, her soul was sold to Satan long ago, and she
is well known for a witch that wants the tar-barrel.
Aye, she has done her work. Maybe she'll be paid
for it and maybe no; but the job is to get you
away and back to your father in the meanwhile,
no that you're to bide long with him. I wuss to
God, my darling, you had never quitted St. Kilda,
and the more fool was I to gratify you."

"Had you no, I would never have spoken to you
again "—she emphasized that assertion by pressing
up to him gently—" but now you may take me
away when I have waited for the funeral."

"Aye, I was thinking that, and I'll be there
myself and see that no mischief happens you.
Now that the black business is over none of the
Fraser folk will be caring to seek quarrel with me.
Were it man to man, or but two to one, I would
reck little of it if they did. Yet I would wish you
had another kind of entertainer. But Elspeth

knows nothing of the converse between you and the lady, and if she did I well believe she would be willing to let you go skaithless, were it only to spite Lovat or any other body. She may gather her simples by the starlight and mutter her spells, but she's no a skilled practitioner at the best, and you'll be careful if there be a queer taste in the brose or the bannocks. I fear you must trust yourself a bit to Providence for the day or two, and after that I'll be caution for you myself. Ilk night at this same mirk hour I'll be here to keep tryste with you. If you miss it, I'll come scratching at your door at midnight. The men after their drinking will be sleeping like swine, and as for the auld witch she is deaf as her peat stack."

The rough and unceremonious funeral rites were a fitting close to a stormy life and a gloomy tragedy. There were neither means nor ready hands to make a coffin on the spot. The body, shrouded in a plaid, was strapped on to a pony, to be transported over fifteen long Highland miles of trackless hill to the nearest burial-place. It was not a kirkyard, for kirk there was none. It was the site of a Catholic Chapel or of some saint's hermitage, the foundations of which could still be faintly traced, and it had once been the graveyard of a now deserted hamlet. Jessie followed as the only mourner. Another pony had been caught and haltered for her. The minister of a parish, five and twenty miles in length, had consented to be present; but it was never the custom in Presbyterian Scotland to pray over the grave, and the body was consigned to the dust without a sign of devotion. Yet not in silence, though the hillmen who assisted were awed into decent observance, and ceased the songs and the chatter with which they had beguiled the way. All the day the sky had been black and lowering, and it was hard to trace the blending lines between the dark cloud and the swarthy heather. The ponies had been forced into a jog-trot; the followers, though used to wild weather, cast uneasy glances over their shoulders. The forebodings of the weatherwise were fulfilled. As they began to toss the gravel back into the shallow grave and the first shovelfuls were rattling on the coffin of rough pine planks, the premonitory rumblings of thunder were succeeded by a deafening crash. Blazes of lurid fire lit up the sinister landscape, and flashed a ghastly light on the faces of the startled group. The lightnings ran along the reeking ground and licked the fast-forming pools of water, for the rain descended in floods and torrents. Never had there been such a storm in the memory of living man. And that was Lady Grange's *requiem*, and, as men said afterwards, Lord Lovat's dirge.

    *   *   *   *   *

On Thursday, the 9th of April, 1747, all London was making holiday. Hundreds of thousands had gathered round Tower Hill. The pressure was so great, the eagerness to witness the spectacle so absorbing, that the fall of the scaffolding, when several people were killed and many more injured, passed almost unnoticed. One man, indeed, remarked on it, with constitutional cynicism, and that was the hero of the popular *fête*. For the long course of Lovat had been run, and the venerable intriguer had been tried and convicted. Though his guilt was patent, he might have escaped, for his clansmen and confidants were staunch to their chieftain, and not a man of them would witness against him. But by an appropriate

Nemesis, the chief evidence for the Crown against the man who had betrayed all causes habitually, and in turn, was the arch-traitor, Murray of Broughton. Lovat was doomed at last, and resigned himself to his fate with a dignity that became him better than anything in his life. Who shall say, in that many-minded man, how much was hypocrisy and how much self-delusion! It is difficult to believe in the wearing a mask when the quickest of intellects, susceptible to religion or superstition, is deliberately facing the plunge into eternity. There is the solemn interview with the chaplain of the Sardinian embassy when he declared that he rested on the Rock of Ages, and that "he adhered to the Rock on which Christ built His Church." There is his dying speech on the scaffold, his last in this world, "*Dulce et decorum est pro patriâ mori.*" As Lovat had a quick perception of the ridiculous, it is hard to believe he was not sincere. He had been deceiving others all his life, and like other statesmen and diplomatists, he may have found it advisable to begin by deluding himself, and carried the practice of self-deception to a fine art.

U

Among the many spectators was one old man,
who had been on the ground almost from daybreak.
There had been a time when his birth, rank, and
reputation would have secured him every consideration from those who had the directing of the tragedy.
Now, he shrank from the society of his equals or
superiors, and had been accustomed to skulk in bye-
streets and to shift for his living and lodging. Those
who had known Lord Grange when pride still
mastered remorse, and when he trod the causeway
of the Edinburgh High Street with unlowered crest
and unruffled dignity, would scarcely have recognized
him now, in the shambling figure, with the bloated
face, with the undressed peruke and the thread-
bare garments. He had found a place against a
barrier, immediately behind the line of soldiers,
which saved him from being crushed. So he witnessed the spectacle from the front row of the pit,
with ease and ample leisure for reflection. What
a many memories it recalled! How perversely, at
the partings of the ways, he had always taken the
wrong turning! How often the counsels of Lovat
had swayed the fatal decisions! Yet why should
he accuse anyone but himself? What could he

blame, except his own feebleness. He might have
been anything, and now he was nothing. Already
he was anticipating the heart-searchings of the lost,
on whom has been passed the irrevocable sentence.
He thought his old friend had recognized him and
cast him one of those quizzical glances, which
brought back the carouses at " Fortune's " or
" Walker's." That might have been fancy. * * *

The axe fell, and between him and his old ally,
for the time being, a great gulf was fixed. He dared
not follow that dark spirit in its flight, or imagine
its appeal to the supreme tribunal. His case, like
Simon's, must soon be judged—and the pleadings
would be terribly similar—in a Court where sophis-
tries were of no avail, and where no counsel are
retained to confound the issues. He waited till the
dense multitude had dispersed; then he bent his
steps, almost mechanically, to the tavern in Fleet
Street, where he was better known than trusted. The
Lord Grange got scrimp credit from the familiar
cockney taverner, because he was a sort of celebrity
or notoriety—a walking advertisement. He saw city
bloods and shop apprentices nod and wink towards
him, and the humiliation had sunk into his soul.

His family pride rose up in arms, but his belly was
craving for food, and his thirst for drink and oblivion
was unquenchable. So James Erskine truckled to
the landlord who bullied him, and when far gone
towards the small hours would accept a glass or a
quart pot from the vulgar mockers who were making
themselves sport. This day, thanks to one of the
rare remittances from Scotland in answer to begging
applications to kinsmen and old acquaintances,
he chanced to have a few shillings in his pocket.
He could afford to sit apart and indulge his
melancholy. His mood was black enough, and he
never felt more despairing. Suicide was a natural
resource, but he knew it was out of the question.
The old Judge had thought it over long ago, and
come to the conclusion that he dared not press for
a hearing at the supreme Court before he was
summoned to appear. He could only wait, though,
in the excess of his apprehensions, the suspense was
crushingly intolerable. Long ere now he had lost
all force of will, and a change in his drifting habits
was out of the question. Then a drawer brought
him a letter which had been lying neglected at the
bar. There were foreign postmarks, and it came

from the Colonies. He opened it listlessly, but awakened to interest, when he saw that, by a strange coincidence, it bore relation to the event of the day.

Jessie wrote from a plantation on the James River, Virginia. She prayed his forgiveness for not having communicated with him long before now. She was no great penwoman, and she had scrupled to trouble his lordship; but now it had been borne in upon her that she ought to write. "If you have ever given us a thought, I trust you did not believe us ungrateful, for night and morning we have been blessing you on our bended knees. We are more than well-to-do for folk like us, and likely to be richer. God has helped us in our struggles and blessed our substance. May He guard us from all snares and temptations. The bairns are stout and healthy; we are happy and full of hope; and we owe everything to your lordship's liberality. You have been even over-generous as to your lady's dying bequest; her forgiveness is sealed to you and the reward is sure."

"God grant it," ejaculated Grange, doubtfully,

" but if she knew all, maybe she would have been less effusive, for what I did was done chiefly for my own sake. No, there is never a solitary action I can look back upon with any satisfaction."

For once he paid his score on the spot, and leaving long before his accustomed hour, stalked out of the tavern in moody thought.

It is to be feared that his lordship's doubts were justified. Some years afterwards, he entered into other nuptials, but he was destined to be unfortunate in matrimony. The second Lady Grange was mistress of a coffee-house in the Haymarket, more addicted to the bottle and far more of a termagant than the unhappy Rachel Chiesley of Dalry. Her violent temper and coarse manners fretted the susceptibilities of the degraded but still sensitive gentleman at every turn; and the woman, although illiterate and densely dull, had wit enough to know where to wound him. She doled out the money for which he had married so stingily that he could seldom drown his misery in drink. The last days of Lord Grange were a long drawn-out martyrdom; he sometimes would envy the repose of Lovat, who at least had assurance of his fate in eternity, and it is best to drop a veil over the death-bed of the man who had aspired to be High Minister for Scotland and hold the scales between the contending factions in the State.

BRADBURY, AGNEW & CO. PRINTERS, LONDON AND TONBRIDGE.

POPULAR NOVELS.

Each Work complete in One Volume, crown 8vo. price Six Shillings.

UNCLE BERNAC: a Memory of the Empire. With 12 full-page Illustrations. By A. CONAN DOYLE.

RODNEY STONE. By A. CONAN DOYLE. With 8 full-page Illustrations.

CLEG KELLY, ARAB OF THE CITY. By S. R. CROCKETT. Thirty-second Thousand.

THE SOWERS. By HENRY SETON MERRIMAN. Fourteenth Edition.

THE WHITE COMPANY. By A. CONAN DOYLE. Seventeenth Edition.

THE LADY GRANGE. By ALEXANDER INNES SHAND.

THE WAYS OF LIFE: Two Stories. By Mrs. OLIPHANT.

CAPTAIN CASTLE: a Tale of the China Seas. By CARLTON DAWE. With a Frontispiece.

THE YOUNG CLANROY: a Romance of the '45. By the Rev. COSMO GORDON LANG.

OUT OF THE DARKNESS. By PERCY FENDALL and FOX RUSSELL.

THE BORDERER. By ADAM LILBURN.

UNDER THE CIRCUMSTANCES. By ARCHIE ARMSTRONG.

GILBERT MURRAY. By A. E. HOUGHTON.

GERALD EVERSLEY'S FRIEND-SHIP; a Study in Real Life. By the Rev. J. E. C. WELLDON. Fourth Edition.

THE WARDLAWS. By E. RENTOUL ESLER.

KATE GRENVILLE. By Lord MONKS-WELL.

DISTURBING ELEMENTS. By MABEL C. BIRCHENOUGH.

IN SEARCH OF QUIET: a Country Journal. By WALTER FRITH.

KINCAID'S WIDOW. By SARAH TYTLER.

THE MARTYRED FOOL. By D. CHRISTIE MURRAY.

A FATAL RESERVATION. By R. O. PROWSE.

THE VAGABONDS. By Mrs. MAR-GARET L. WOODS.

GRANIA: the Story of an Island. By the Hon. EMILY LAWLESS.

THE SIGNORA: a Tale. By PERCY ANDREAE.

STANHOPE OF CHESTER: a Mystery. By PERCY ANDREAE.

THE MASK AND THE MAN. By PERCY ANDREAE.

A WOMAN OF THE WORLD. By F. MABEL ROBINSON.

SIR GEORGE TRESSADY. By Mrs. HUMPHRY WARD. Third Edition.

MARCELLA. By Mrs. HUMPHRY WARD. Sixteenth Edition.

ROBERT ELSMERE. By Mrs. HUM-PHRY WARD. Twenty-seventh Edition.

THE HISTORY OF DAVID GRIEVE. By Mrs. HUMPHRY WARD. Ninth Edition.

A FALLEN IDOL. By F. ANSTEY, Author of 'Vice Versâ' &c.

THE GIANT'S ROBE. By F. ANSTEY, Author of 'Vice Versâ' &c.

THE PARIAH. By F. ANSTEY, Author of 'Vice Versâ' &c.

THE TALKING HORSE: and other Tales. By F. ANSTEY.

NEW GRUB STREET. By GEORGE GISSING, Author of 'Demos' &c.

THYRZA. By George Gissing, Author of 'Demos' &c.

THE NETHER WORLD. By GEORGE GISSING, Author of 'Demos' &c.

DEMOS: a Story of Socialist Life in England. By GEORGE GISSING.

RICHARD CABLE: the Lightshipman. By the Author of 'Mehalah' &c.

THE GAVEROCKS. By the Author of 'Mehalah,' 'John Herring,' &c.

EIGHT DAYS. By R. E. FORREST, Author of 'The Touchstone of Peril.'

A DRAUGHT OF LETHE. By ROY TELLET, Author of 'The Outcasts' &c.

THE RAJAH'S HEIR. By a NEW AUTHOR.

OLD KENSINGTON. By Miss THACK-ERAY.

THE VILLAGE ON THE CLIFF. By Miss THACKERAY.

FIVE OLD FRIENDS AND A YOUNG PRINCE. By Miss THACKERAY.

TO ESTHER, and other Sketches. By Miss THACKERAY.

BLUEBEARD'S KEYS, and other Stories. By Miss THACKERAY.

THE STORY OF ELIZABETH; TWO HOURS; FROM AN ISLAND. By Miss THACKERAY.

TOILERS AND SPINSTERS. By Miss THACKERAY.

MISS ANGEL: FULHAM LAWN. By Miss THACKERAY.

MISS WILLIAMSON'S DIVAGA-TIONS. By Miss THACKERAY.

MRS. DYMOND. By Miss THACKERAY.

LLANALY REEFS. By Lady VERNEY, Author of 'Stone Edge' &c.

LETTICE LISLE. By Lady VERNEY. With 3 Illustrations.

London: SMITH, ELDER, & CO., 15 Waterloo Place.

ILLUSTRATED EDITIONS

OF

POPULAR WORKS.

Handsomely bound in cloth gilt, each volume containing
Four Illustrations. Crown 8vo. 3s. 6d. each.

———◦◦———

THE SMALL HOUSE AT ALLINGTON. By ANTHONY TROLLOPE.

FRAMLEY PARSONAGE. By ANTHONY TROLLOPE.

THE CLAVERINGS. By ANTHONY TROLLOPE.

TRANSFORMATION: a Romance. By NATHANIEL HAWTHORNE.

DOMESTIC STORIES. By the Author of 'John Halifax, Gentleman.'

THE MOORS AND THE FENS. By Mrs. J. H. RIDDELL.

WITHIN THE PRECINCTS. By Mrs. OLIPHANT.

CARITÀ. By Mrs. OLIPHANT.

FOR PERCIVAL. By MARGARET VELEY.

NO NEW THING. By W. E. NORRIS.

LOVE THE DEBT. By RICHARD ASHE KING ('Basil').

WIVES AND DAUGHTERS. By Mrs. GASKELL.

NORTH AND SOUTH. By Mrs. GASKELL.

SYLVIA'S LOVERS. By Mrs. GASKELL.

CRANFORD, and other Stories. By Mrs. GASKELL.

MARY BARTON, and other Stories. By Mrs. GASKELL.

RUTH ; THE GREY WOMAN, and other Stories. By
Mrs. GASKELL.

LIZZIE LEIGH ; A DARK NIGHT'S WORK, and other Stories.
By Mrs. GASKELL.

London : SMITH, ELDER, & CO., 15 Waterloo Place.

WORKS BY F. ANSTEY.

THE TALKING HORSE; and other Tales.
Popular Edition. Crown 8vo. 6s. Cheap Edition. Crown 8vo. limp red cloth, 2s. 6d.

From THE SATURDAY REVIEW.—'A capital set of stories, thoroughly clever and witty, often pathetic, and always humorous.'

From THE ATHENÆUM.—'The grimmest of mortals, in his most surly mood, could hardly resist the fun of "The Talking Horse."'

THE GIANT'S ROBE. Popular Edition. Crown 8vo.
6s. Cheap Edition. Crown 8vo. limp red cloth, 2s. 6d.

From THE PALL MALL GAZETTE. —'The main interest of the book, which is very strong indeed, begins when Vincent returns, when Harold Caffyn discovers the secret, when every page threatens to bring down doom on the head of the miserable Mark. Will he confess? Will he drown himself? Will Vincent denounce him? Will Caffyn inform on him? Will his wife abandon him?—we ask eagerly as we read and cannot cease reading till the puzzle is solved in a series of exciting situations.'

THE PARIAH. Popular Edition. Crown 8vo. 6s. Cheap
Edition. Crown 8vo. limp red cloth, 2s. 6d.

From THE SATURDAY REVIEW.—'In "The Pariah" we are more than ever struck by the sharp intuitive perception and the satirical balancing of judgment which makes the author's writings such extremely entertaining reading. There is not a dull page—we might say, not a dull sentence—in it. . . . The girls are delightfully drawn, especially the bewitching Margot and the childish Lettice. Nothing that polish and finish, cleverness, humour, wit, and sarcasm can give us is left out.'

VICE VERSÂ; or, a Lesson to Fathers. Cheap
Edition. Crown 8vo. limp red cloth, 2s. 6d.

From THE SATURDAY REVIEW.—'If ever there was a book made up from beginning to end of laughter, and yet not a comic book, or a "merry" book, or a book of jokes, or a book of pictures, or a jest book, or a tomfool book, but a perfectly sober and serious book, in the reading of which a sober man may laugh without shame from beginning to end, it is the book called "Vice Versâ; or, a Lesson to Fathers." . . We close the book, recommending it very earnestly to all fathers in the first instance, and their sons, nephews, uncles, and male cousins next.'

A FALLEN IDOL. Cheap Edition. Crown 8vo. limp
red cloth, 2s. 6d.

From THE TIMES.—'Will delight the multitudinous public that laughed over "Vice Versâ.". . . The boy who brings the accursed image to Champion's house, Mr. Bales, the artist's factotum, and above all Mr. Yarker, the ex-butler who has turned policeman, are figures whom it is as pleasant to meet as it is impossible to forget.'

LYRE AND LANCET. With 24 Full-page Illustrations.
Square 16mo. 3s.

From THE SPEAKER.—'Mr. Anstey has surpassed himself in "Lyre and Lancet." . . . One of the brightest and most entertaining bits of comedy we have had for many a day.'

From THE GLOBE.—'The little book is amusing from beginning to end.'

From THE SCOTSMAN.—'The story makes most delightful reading, full of quiet fun.'

London : SMITH, ELDER, & CO., 15 Waterloo Place.

RURAL ENGLAND.

WORKS BY THE LATE RICHARD JEFFERIES.

THE GAMEKEEPER AT HOME; or, Sketches of Natural History and Rural Life. New Edition, with all the Illustrations of the former Edition. Crown 8vo. 5s.

'Delightful sketches. The lover of the country can hardly fail to be fascinated whenever he may happen to open the pages. It is a book to read and keep for reference, and should be on the shelves of every country gentleman's library.'—SATURDAY REVIEW.

ROUND ABOUT A GREAT ESTATE. New Edition. Crown 8vo. 5s.

'To read a book of his is really like taking a trip into some remote part of the country, where the surroundings of life remain very much what they were thirty or forty years ago. Mr. Jefferies has made up a very pleasant volume.'—THE GLOBE.

WILD LIFE IN A SOUTHERN COUNTY. New Edition. Crown 8vo. 6s.

'A volume which is worthy of a place beside White's "Selborne." In closeness of observation, in power of giving a picture far beyond the power of a mere word painter, he is the equal of the Selborne rector—perhaps his superior. This is a book to read and to treasure.'
THE ATHENÆUM.

THE AMATEUR POACHER. New Edition. Crown 8vo. 5s.

' Unsurpassed in power of observation and sympathy with natural objects by anything that has appeared since the days of Gilbert White.'—DAILY NEWS.
' We have rarely met with a book in which so much that is entertaining is combined with matter of real practical worth.'—THE GRAPHIC.

HODGE AND HIS MASTERS. New Edition. Cr. 8vo. 7s. 6d.

' The one great charm of Mr. Jefferies' writings may be summed up in the single word "graphic." He has a rare power of description, and in "Hodge and his Masters" we find plenty of good reading.'—STANDARD.
'Mr. Jefferies knows his ground well and thoroughly, and writes with much of his wonted straightforwardness and assurance. ... Pleasant and easy reading throughout.'—ATHENÆUM.

WOODLAND, MOOR, AND STREAM; being the Notes of a Naturalist. Edited by J. A. OWEN. Third Edition. Crown 8vo. 5s.

' As a specimen of word-painting, the description of the quaint old fishing village close to the edge of the North Kent marshes can hardly be surpassed. ... The book is capitally written, full of good stories, and thoroughly commendable.'—THE ATHENÆUM.

FOREST TITHES; and other Studies from Nature. By the Author of ' Woodland, Moor, and Stream,' &c. Edited by J. A. OWEN. Crown 8vo. 5s.

' The book should be read. It is full of the spirit of the South Country, and as we read it we seem to hear again the clack of the millwheel, the cry of the water-fowl, and the splash of fish.'—SPECTATOR.

ALL THE YEAR WITH NATURE. By P. ANDERSON GRAHAM. Crown 8vo. 5s.

' Of the 28 papers composing the volume there is not one which does not brim over with love of Nature, observation of her by-paths, and power of sympathetic expression.'—OBSERVER.

London: SMITH, ELDER, & CO., 15 Waterloo Place.

ILLUSTRATED EDITION

OF THE

LIFE AND WORKS OF CHARLOTTE BRONTË

(CURRER BELL), AND HER SISTERS,

EMILY and ANNE BRONTË

(ELLIS AND ACTON BELL).

In SEVEN VOLUMES, large crown 8vo. handsomely bound in cloth price 5s. per volume.

Vignette Title-page Illustration to ' Jane Eyre.'

CONTENTS OF THE VOLUMES.

1. **JANE EYRE.** By CHARLOTTE BRONTË. With Five Illustrations.
2. **SHIRLEY.** By CHARLOTTE BRONTË. With Five Illustrations.
3. **VILLETTE.** By CHARLOTTE BRONTË. With Five Illustrations.
4. **THE PROFESSOR, and POEMS.** By CHARLOTTE BRONTË. With Poems by her Sisters and Father. With Five Illustrations.
5. **WUTHERING HEIGHTS.** By EMILY BRONTË. **AGNES GREY.** By ANNE BRONTË. With a Preface and Biographical Notice of both Authors by CHARLOTTE BRONTË. With Five Illustrations.
6. **THE TENANT OF WILDFELL HALL.** By ANNE BRONTË. With Five Illustrations.
7. **LIFE OF CHARLOTTE BRONTË.** By Mrs. GASKELL. With Seven Illustrations.

** The Volumes are also to be had in small post 8vo. limp cloth, or cloth boards, gilt top, price 2s. 6d. each: and in small fcp. 8vo. bound in half-cloth, with Frontispiece to each volume, cut or uncut edges, price 1s. 6d. each; or the Set bound in cloth, with gilt top, in gold-lettered cloth case, 12s. 6d.

London : SMITH, ELDER, & CO., 15 Waterloo Place.

ILLUSTRATED EDITION

OF

MRS. GASKELL'S NOVELS & TALES

In SEVEN VOLUMES, bound in cloth, each containing
Four Illustrations, price 3s. 6d. each.

Reduction to nearly one-third size of one of the Illustrations to 'Sylvia's Lovers.'

' " What ails yo' at me !" said he, beseechingly.'

CONTENTS OF THE VOLUMES.

1. WIVES AND DAUGHTERS.   2. NORTH AND SOUTH.
3. SYLVIA'S LOVERS.
4. CRANFORD.

Company Manners—The Well of Pen-Morpha—The Heart of John Middleton—Traits and Stories of the Huguenots—Six Weeks at Heppenheim—The Squire's Story—Libbie Marsh's Three Eras—Curious if True—The Moorland Cottage—The Sexton's Hero—Disappearances—Right at Last—The Manchester Marriage—Lois the Witch—The Crooked Branch.

5. MARY BARTON.

Cousin Phillis—My French Master—The Old Nurse's Story—Bessy's Troubles at Home—Christmas Storms and Sunshine.

6. RUTH.

The Grey Woman—Morton Hall—Mr. Harrison's Confessions—Hand and Heart.

7. LIZZIE LEIGH.

A Dark Night's Work—Round the Sofa—My Lady Ludlow—An Accursed Race—The Doom of the Griffiths—Half a Lifetime Ago—The Poor Clare—The Half-Brothers.

*** The volumes are also to be had in small post 8vo. limp cloth, or cloth boards, gilt top, price 2s. 6d. each: and in Eight Volumes, small fcp. 8vo. bound in half-cloth, cut or uncut edges, price 1s. 6d. each ; or the Set bound in cloth, with gilt top, in gold-lettered cloth case, 14s.

London: SMITH, ELDER, & CO., 15 Waterloo Place.

WORKS
OF
ELIZABETH BARRETT BROWNING.

—◆—

THE POETICAL WORKS OF ELIZABETH BARRETT BROWNING.
UNIFORM EDITION.

Six Volumes, in set binding, small crown 8vo. 5s. each.

Volume 6.—'AURORA LEIGH'—can also be had bound as a separate volume.

This Edition is uniform with the 17-Volume edition of Mr. Robert Browning's Works. It contains the following Portraits and Illustrations:—

Portrait of Elizabeth Barrett Moulton-Barrett at the age of nine.
Coxhoe Hall, County of Durham.
Portrait of Elizabeth Barrett Moulton-Barrett in early youth.
Portrait of Mrs. Browning, Rome, February 1859.
Hope End, Herefordshire.
Sitting Room of Casa Guidi, Florence.
'May's Love,'—Facsimile of Mrs. Browning's Handwriting.
Portrait of Mrs. Browning, Rome, March 1859.
Portrait of Mrs. Browning, Rome, 1861.
The Tomb of Mrs. Browning in the Cemetery at Florence.

A SELECTION FROM THE POETRY OF ELIZABETH BARRETT BROWNING.

FIRST SERIES, crown 8vo. 3s. 6d.   SECOND SERIES, crown 8vo. 3s. 6d.

POEMS.

Small fcp. 8vo. half-cloth, cut or uncut edges, 1s.

EXTRACT FROM PREFATORY NOTE BY MR. ROBERT BROWNING.

'In a recent "Memoir of Elizabeth Barrett Browning," by JOHN H. INGRAM, it is observed that "such essays on her personal history as have appeared, either in England or elsewhere, are replete with mistakes or misstatements." For these he proposes to substitute "a correct if short memoir:" but, kindly and appreciative as may be Mr. Ingram's performance, there occur not a few passages in it equally "mistaken and misstated."'

London: SMITH, ELDER, & CO., 15 Waterloo Place.

www.ingramcontent.com/pod-product-compliance
Lightning Source LLC
Chambersburg PA
CBHW021033030726
47496CB00006B/1517